"Do you like it?"

John slid the fork from Anne's mouth.

The rich dessert melted on Anne's tongue, fulfilling his every promise of a delectable treat, but it was hard to swallow when he was looking at her so intently. "It's heaven."

"No," he corrected, taking her in his arms. "This is heaven."

And it *was* heaven, Anne thought. One second of his kiss and she knew this man, this time, was different. She was aware only of his long, drugging kisses and her own sighs and of the fact that this man wanted her... wanted her desperately.

But she couldn't let herself forget time and place... or the scandal that stood between them. "But your family—" she managed.

"You still want to go back?" His throaty whisper was a demand. Without waiting for a response, his mouth covered hers again.

Dear Reader,

For most of us, Fourth of July means town parades, family picnics and fireworks lighting up the night sky. But Anne Haynes and John Westfield make fireworks of their own in Cathy Gillen Thacker's *Home Free,* July's Calendar of Romance title.

In A Calendar of Romance, you can experience all the passion and excitement of falling in love during each month's special holiday. Join us next month when Judith Arnold brings back sweet memories of summer love, of those long, hot days... and even hotter nights, in #449 *Opposing Camps,* August's Calendar of Romance title.

We hope you're enjoying all the books in A Calendar of Romance, coming to you one per month, all year, only in American Romance. We'd love to hear from you!

Debra Matteucci
Senior Editor & Editorial Coordinator
Harlequin Books
300 E. 42nd St., 6th floor
New York, NY 10017

CATHY GILLEN THACKER

HOME FREE

Harlequin Books

TORONTO • NEW YORK • LONDON
AMSTERDAM • PARIS • SYDNEY • HAMBURG
STOCKHOLM • ATHENS • TOKYO • MILAN
MADRID • WARSAW • BUDAPEST • AUCKLAND

If you purchased this book without a cover you should be aware that this book is stolen property. It was reported as "unsold and destroyed" to the publisher, and neither the author nor the publisher has received any payment for this "stripped book."

Published July 1992

ISBN 0-373-16445-9

HOME FREE

Copyright © 1992 by Cathy Gillen Thacker. All rights reserved. Except for use in any review, the reproduction or utilization of this work in whole or in part in any form by any electronic, mechanical or other means, now known or hereafter invented, including xerography, photocopying and recording, or in any information storage or retrieval system, is forbidden without the permission of the publisher, Harlequin Enterprises Limited, 225 Duncan Mill Road, Don Mills, Ontario, Canada M3B 3K9.

All the characters in this book have no existence outside the imagination of the author and have no relation whatsoever to anyone bearing the same name or names. They are not even distantly inspired by any individual known or unknown to the author, and all incidents are pure invention.

® are Trademarks registered in the United States Patent and Trademark Office and in other countries.

Printed in U.S.A.

Chapter One

"I've already tried to find out what I could on my own and got, basically, nowhere," the well-groomed teenage boy said, raking both hands through his inky-black hair in a gesture of frustration. "If you don't help me, Ms. Haynes, I don't know what I'll do."

"Slow down," Anne advised her young visitor. He'd come in without an appointment, and before she could do much more than elicit a name from him, he had immediately hit her with a barrage of confusing facts and urgent pleas, none of which, unfortunately, were making very much sense. Worse, his sense of timing was the pits.

With reluctance, she pushed aside the manila folder of information with the decade-old black-and-white military identification photos she had been poring over. She struggled to keep her mind off her own private difficulties and the package. "Tim, is it?"

He nodded, his almond-shaped eyes scanning her dark hair and blue eyes. "Tim Westfield," he confirmed, in an American accent that seemed slightly at odds with his uniquely Amerasian countenance.

"Have a seat, Tim." She waited until he had eased his lanky frame into a chair. An Amerasian herself who had migrated to the United States when she was five, she knew how it felt to look as if you hailed from the other side of the world, but act and talk and feel as American as Apple Pie. Or, she amended silently, as American as most people would allow you to feel. To those for whom looks were everything, people like her and Tim would never entirely fit in. And that was a shame because she knew she—and probably Tim, too—wanted nothing more than to belong, in deep, intrinsic ways that most Americans took entirely for granted.

Satisfied Tim had calmed down, she settled herself on the edge of her desk. "Now start at the beginning again."

"Okay." He took a deep breath, knitted his hands together tightly and then dangled them prayerfully between his spread knees. In jeans and a striped red-and-white long-sleeved T-shirt, with his long, stylishly cut jet-black hair and flawless golden skin, he looked every bit the privileged child of wealthy parents. "I'm adopted and I'm here because I want to hire you to find my birth parents."

"Whoa," Anne said, holding up a hand stop-sign fashion before he could go any further. She scanned him again from the top of his head to the toes of his Top-Siders. "How old are you?" Judging from his sockless state on a chilly day in early May, not very old. Anyone older would have had enough sense to wear some socks when the temperature was hovering in the upper forties.

"Eighteen. I just had a birthday last week." Tim removed his wallet from his back pocket. Flipping it open, he showed Anne his New Hampshire driver's license. "That means I can look without parental consent."

Which probably also meant that his adoptive parents didn't want him to look for his birth parents. Anne didn't want to put herself in the middle of a family quarrel if she could help it. It was bad enough she was fighting with her family about her own need to know. Her continuing search was just now, after years of effort, beginning to reap information. However, she respected Tim's right to look into his past. Aware he probably had nowhere else to go, she said finally, "All right. I'll take your case and do everything in my power to help you."

Tim shot her a grateful smile. "Great," he said. "I don't know a whole lot about my early life, except that I was put in a Catholic orphanage by my mother shortly after my birth. I ended up living there for about a year and a half and was brought back from Korea by my adoptive father about a year after his tour. He was a West Point grad, who was stationed in Korea twenty years ago." Briefly, Jim's eyes reflected loss. He continued in a soft, grief-stricken voice, "You've probably heard of him. Senator Frank Westfield..."

The late United States senator from New Hampshire, Anne finished silently. His family was to New Hampshire politics what the Kennedys were to Massachusetts'!

For a second, she was silent. Doubtless, the powerful, political Westfield family would not want Tim here with her. If they had wanted him to discover his roots, they would have helped him untangle the miles of red tape between the two governments. Perhaps they were right to not help. Tim's father, the late Senator Frank Westfield, had died suddenly three months ago of an aneurysm, and Tim was perhaps too vulnerable to be thinking straight now.

Anne didn't want to take advantage of his grief; she didn't want to help him do now anything he would later regret. And yet at eighteen, this was his right.

Aware he was waiting for some response from her, she found her voice and picked up the threads of the conversation. "Yes, of course I know of your father, Tim. I even helped vote him into the Senate. I also heard about his death." Her tone colored sympathetically. "I'm sorry." She knew that whether he admitted it to himself or not, Tim had to still be reeling from the tragedy. News reports said the entire Westfield family was devastated.

"Thanks," Tim said. He looked away briefly, as if fighting for control. He knotted his hands together until the knuckles turned white and continued in a thick voice, "I miss him, you know?"

Anne nodded, wishing she could do more for him now. She hated feeling helpless almost more than she hated feeling as if she didn't belong. And she didn't belong—not here in New Hampshire, not back in Vietnam where she'd been born twenty-eight years ago, not anywhere.

Tim scuffed his shoes on the carpeted floor beneath him. "It probably seems like I'm heartless or something. Me, wanting to look for my real mom and dad. Now, of all times—"

"No, it doesn't, Tim," she said gently. "Most adopted children want to find their birth parents." Naturally, now that his adoptive father was gone, his curiosity about his natural parents was even more intense, she thought.

"I feel like I have to know, Ms. Haynes, like I won't ever really know who I am until I find out who he was and what happened to my mom. To be fair, I already have a pretty good idea why she gave me up. Korean women were shamed for having a baby out of wedlock, an Amerasian baby would have been even worse. She was unmarried, so there's no way she could have kept me. No way."

Anne nodded. God, how she understood Tim. But she had had no one to turn to, nowhere to go for help, no specialized agency such as her own to consult. Now, after eight years, she finally had a name and a social security number for the Navy helicopter ground crewman who had been involved with her mother. She had photos of him, taken about the time she was conceived. And one day soon, she would confront him, face-to-face. She would find out why he had not kept any of the promises he had made....

"Anyway, that's why I'm here now," Tim continued. "I always promised myself that when I was eighteen and didn't have to hurt anyone by asking permission that I would look."

Anne studied him, wanting to make certain she wasn't inadvertently taking advantage of Tim's grief-ridden state in her drive to get to the truth. "If your adoptive father hadn't died, would you still be doing this now, or would you have waited a bit?"

Tim met her eyes. "I'd still be looking now," he said. "I'd still want to know what happened back then...why my American father didn't marry my Korean mother and how he could just leave her like that." Tim shrugged, searching visibly for a way to reassure himself. "Of course, maybe my dad didn't know my mother was pregnant," he theorized hopefully.

And maybe, Anne thought, he had known but had chosen to leave his Korean girlfriend and infant son and go back to the States, anyway. Many servicemen had reached out to a woman in their loneliness, but then realized that was all it was when it was time to go home.

"It could take a very long time," she warned, being as honest and forthright with him as she was with all her clients. "Maybe even years." In her case, it had taken eight years of letter writing to nurses and doctors all over Saigon. Eight years of dead ends and disappointments and false leads.

And then today, a letter had come. Someone who had known her Vietnamese mother had been located at the State Department in Washington. That someone remembered that her father's name was Robert Ryan and that he'd been a chopper ground crewman in the Navy.

Against regulations, her contact at the Department of Defense had given her the black-and-white military photographs and the social security number. From there, she was on her own. She knew she could find him now. She was so close and so scared. But no less determined to confront him.

"I don't care how long it takes or what I have to go through or how much money I have to spend," Tim was saying passionately. "I just want to find out."

"Do you know anything about your birth mother?" Anne asked.

He shook his head sadly. "No. Nothing. All I know is that I was adopted out of a Catholic orphanage in Seoul."

Anne reached behind her for a notepad and pen. "Do you know the name of it?"

Tim shook his head. "No. I asked my adoptive mother. She said she never knew, that my dad took care of everything."

Anne paused. "Does your adoptive mother know you want to find your birth parents?"

"No," Tim said hurriedly, leaning forward in his chair. "And I don't want her to know. My dad's death hit us all pretty hard. Mom's still pretty fragile. News of this would only upset her."

"Then why are you doing it?" Anne probed gently, hearing the love he had for Mrs. Westfield.

"Because I have to know for my peace of mind," he answered honestly. "Maybe that's not something you can understand—"

"Actually," Anne interjected, thinking of her own situation, "it is." At Tim's astonished look, she confided warmly, "I'm adopted, too. My father was an American serviceman, stationed in Vietnam during the war." He had left when she was two, promising her mother he would come back someday and get them both. But he never had. Her mother had worried that the man Anne now knew was Robert Ryan was dead. Anne had worried and grieved over her lost daddy, too.

"So you were adopted when you were a baby?" Tim asked, pleased they had that in common.

Anne nodded. "When I was five."

"So you probably have some memories of your birth parents, right?"

"Of my mother." Anne remembered the beautiful woman with the dark hair and dark eyes. She also remembered her mother's sadness and sense of betrayal. She remembered her mother going to work as a practical nurse at the hospital during the days, and later becoming ill. Anne had few memories of her preschool years, but she did recall the photo of her serviceman father that had been set up like a shrine in their small one-room apartment. Anne had just received the same photo in the mail.

"You don't have any memories of your birth father?" Tim asked.

"None," Anne affirmed. There were only the stories her mother had told her, of how kind and loving and wonderful he was. But if he'd been all those things, why hadn't he ever come to get them, as he had promised? Why had her mother died brokenhearted? Why had she been shipped off to a strange albeit loving family in the States for adoption after her mother's death, instead of to her loving father?

For years, she had looked for answers. And now that she had found the key that would unlock all those mysteries, she was unbearably excited and yet afraid of what she might find... afraid her father might not want her now, either.

Forcing herself to be realistic, she warned, "You might not find a happy ending, Tim."

"I know that." At her cautioning words, he stiffened defensively. "But I also know I might. And it's a chance I'm willing to take." He frowned thoughtfully, adding, "I even thought of asking my ex-aunt, Melinda Parker. She writes for the Concord paper, you know. But then I decided not to 'cause even after two years things are still pretty dicey between Melinda and my uncle John."

Tim's "uncle John" was currently running for Governor and was considered one of the most handsome and eligible men in the state of New Hampshire. "What do you mean?" Anne asked.

Tim shrugged. "You know how it is with people who've gotten divorced. I mean, they still talk, but sometimes the way they look at each other tells me there are still hard feelings. Like they feel they let each other down. So I figured she probably wouldn't want to do anything like that for me. Not that she'd have time to do me any big favors, anyway. She's pretty busy with her job."

"Your instincts are right. I don't think it'd be a good idea to go to a newspaper for help, Tim, not about something as private as this. If even the tiniest bit of information got into the wrong hands it could be disastrous, not just for you but for your entire family."

"You mean your search might turn up something bad?" he asked, sending her a wary look.

Anne shrugged. "There's always that possibility." Anne felt an obligation to be brutally honest. "I've had a couple of cases in the past that have turned out badly." Regrettably so.

"What do you mean?"

"In one case, the birth mother didn't want to be found and rejected the child. In another, the natural father, a serviceman during the war, didn't want to acknowledge the daughter he'd abandoned because he'd been married to a woman in the States when his Amerasian child was conceived." She swallowed hard, thinking of the possible parallel to her own situation. "The marriage broke up when the story of his previous affair came out. The father and the daughter he'd abandoned never did reconcile."

It had been a mess and everyone involved had gotten hurt, so much so that Anne still had nightmares about it from time to time, so much so that she still couldn't rid herself of the guilt and the knowledge that in that particular case, at least, she would have been better off leaving well enough alone.

"Are you trying to say that might happen to me?" Tim asked, his expression remaining determined but wary.

Anne sighed. "I'm trying to tell you there are no guarantees. I'd be happy to try to help you, Tim. I just can't promise you a happy ending and I want you to know that going in."

"But you have had happy endings," Tim ascertained pointedly after a moment. "Cases where parent and child found each other and liked each other and all that."

"Oh, yes," Anne said, her mood lightening as the memories of those cases flooded in. She smiled. "Those are the cases that keep me going." And in fact, of the one hundred and thirty-three reunions she had managed to bring about in the last eight years, only two of them had turned out badly. Maybe that was luck. And maybe it was to be expected, she didn't know. She did know she was providing a service people were hard-pressed to find elsewhere. And she wasn't in it for the money—there was very little profit involved—but for the satisfaction it brought her when she did help someone trace their roots and reunite them with their natural parents.

"I don't care about the risks," Tim said finally, giving her a resolute look.

Anne understood what he was saying all too well. Those particular sentiments were what had prompted her to start her grass-roots agency, Answers, Inc.

"I just want you to know what you're getting into," she said. "You're from a very prominent family."

The Westfield political dynasty was known worldwide. And as such they were prey for every newspaper, magazine, and television show in the country. Not to mention the tabloids. Add to that mix the fact that one of Tim's uncles, John Westfield, had just won the primary and was currently running for Governor of New Hampshire, and it could turn out to be a very tricky situation.

Tim looked taken aback, as if he hadn't considered that being a Westfield was a source of many potential problems. "Your services are confidential, aren't they?"

"Very," Anne affirmed, knowing any secret he told her would go no further than her own one-woman office.

"Then what's the problem?"

"None, I guess—" Anne replied, giving him a last searching glance "—as long as you're sure this is what you want."

"I am," he said firmly. He gave her an engaging grin. "My only question is where, when, and how do we begin?"

"JOHN, I've got to talk to you to right away," Gloria Westfield began, barging into his office at campaign headquarters one week later. "Oh, I'm sorry," she said quickly, seeing he'd been busy dictating letters to his executive assistant, Lily Carrington. "I guess I should have knocked, but this latest trouble with the kids has me so rattled..."

Everything was rattling his sister-in-law these days, John thought with a weary sigh, not just her four extremely bright but rambunctious teenagers.

A welcoming smile on his face, he crossed the room and gave her a brief, spirit-bolstering hug hello. He knew he shouldn't feel resentful of Gloria for leaning on him so heavily these days, but the hell of it was, he did. Maybe because it was time Gloria began picking up the pieces of her life. He knew if she didn't do it now, she might never do it. As devoted as he had been to his brother, and as much as he loved his three nieces and one nephew, he didn't want to take Frank's place and Gloria's, too, simply because his brother's widow refused to try harder to cope.

Twenty-three-year-old Lily remained where she was, her steno pad still in hand. As astute about people as ever, she looked from John to Gloria then back to him, as if trying to read the situation. "If this is personal," she began awkwardly, clearly not wanting to intrude.

Gloria shot Lily an apologetic look and sighed, her tense body language all but commanding Lily to leave. "It is. Very."

"Well, then—" Lily began. Ever the capable assistant, she was already up and backing out the door "—I'll make sure the two of you are not disturbed."

John thanked Lily. The door shut behind her.

Stepping back from his sister-in-law's side, John took a closer look at Gloria. Although her makeup was as artfully applied as ever, her bleached blond hair carefully coiffed into its usual short, sophisticated style, he could tell she'd been crying. A woman whose whole life had revolved around her husband and his career, she had been devastated when his older brother had died. Remembering how much she had loved his brother lessened his feelings of resentment. If it was still hard for him, on a daily basis, to be without Frank, how must it be for Frank's widow?

"What is it, Gloria?" he said gently, his heart going out to her once again.

"It's Tim this time." Reaching into her purse, Gloria pulled out a canceled check stub. "This came to the house today in the mail with Tim's canceled checks. I opened his bank statement by mistake, thinking it was mine. He only wrote two checks last month. This was one of them."

John glanced down and saw a check for one hundred dollars, written to Answers, Inc. It was dated the previous week. Turning it over, he saw it had been endorsed by Anne Haynes. Both the name and the business were unfamiliar to him. "Answers, Inc." He repeated the name in mystification. "What is it?"

Tears filled Gloria's eyes. "It's an agency that specializes in locating the American fathers of Amerasian children."

Shock held John motionless for several seconds. He had always known this would happen, of course, but he had prayed against it, chiefly because of the damage that could be done to his family and his campaign if the truth about Tim's early life ever surfaced. "Has

Tim said anything about this to you?" John asked incredulously, unwilling to believe that Tim would hurt his adoptive mother this way. His nephew had always seemed so happy, bright and outgoing. He was so much a member of the gregarious Westfield clan that there were times when it was hard to remember he was adopted.

"No, not a word, not lately." Gloria shook her head despairingly, knowing nothing of the depths of John's fear, or how hard it was for him not to be completely honest with her. "But then he hasn't really talked much to any of us since Frank died." Gloria turned away. One arm was folded tightly at her waist; the other hand fingered her pearls idly. She paced past John's personal computer and to the window overlooking the business district in Concord. "I knew he was mourning his father, John—" Her voice broke. "We all have been. But for him to go and do something like this—what does he hope to gain? What have I done to make him feel he has to go elsewhere for love?"

John reached out for her. Drawing her into his arms, he held her while she sobbed. It would be so easy if he could tell her the truth. And Tim, too. But he couldn't. The truth would destroy them. It would destroy his whole family.

Turning his thoughts back to Gloria's immediate problem, he searched for a way to console her. Tim's actions weren't all that unusual. Nor were they necessarily linked to the dangerous deceptions in the past,

John reassured himself firmly. "He is eighteen, Gloria. Maybe we should have expected this."

Gloria shook her head vigorously and withdrew from his arms. "No," she said, dabbing at her eyes with a soggy tissue. "If Frank were still alive, I know he never would have pursued this, John. I know it."

John wasn't so sure. "What do you want me to do?"

"I want you to stop him, talk to him and make him see that this isn't the right thing to do."

John stared at the canceled check and the graceful, fluid lines of the signed endorsement on the back. Anne Haynes, it read. Anne Haynes. Ever the pragmatist, he wondered what an American would be able to find out about something that had happened halfway across the world, years ago. He knew the records surrounding Tim's birth had been sealed; Frank had seen to that prior to the adoption. Frank had feared if they weren't that he might be leaving their nationally prominent family open to blackmail someday. He had feared what was happening now, John realized uncomfortably.

John knew it was up to him now to make sure nothing volatile or destructive was uncovered now. "I thought you and Frank didn't know anything about Tim's father, other than that he was an American soldier," John remarked casually. He hoped this was still so, that Tim's search had yielded zilch thus far.

"We didn't. Neither did the orphanage. Apparently—-" Gloria's artfully made-up eyes filled with tears again. "Apparently his birth mother had a number of G.I. lovers, or at least that was what she told the orphanage."

This was news to John; he recalled Frank telling them all only that the father was unknown, the mother a young and unmarried Korean girl who had given up her baby to the nuns in the hopes it would be given a good, loving home. He hadn't realized Frank and Gloria had talked further, or that Frank had made up more lies to expound on those he had already told, in his efforts to protect Tim's father.

"Are you saying that Frank told you Tim's mother was a prostitute?" he asked incredulously, unable to believe his brother had gone that far, or that anyone in his or her right mind could even remotely connect the healthy, well-bred, energetic Tim with anything remotely seedy.

"That's just it," Gloria whispered, looking as stricken as John felt, "we don't know who or what she was...."

That wasn't exactly true, John knew. Because he and Frank both knew. As well as several others... But Frank had wanted a baby. He had wanted a son, and he hadn't cared he'd had to adopt, or that the baby had been Amerasian. He had fallen in love with little Tim the first time he'd visited the orphanage and found the little boy, gurgling and cooing happily in his crib. He had vowed then to bring the boy home, even if it meant lying to government officials, bribing countless others, and using every bit of Westfield influence to cut through the miles of bureaucratic red tape. And he, barely twenty at the time, had helped because he would have done anything for his sainted older brother. He still would.

"The orphanage officials wanted her to remain anonymous and we agreed," Gloria continued emotionally, oblivious to John's traitorous thoughts. "At the time it didn't matter to me. All I cared about was that Tim was healthy."

And Tim had been healthy, resoundingly so, John remembered.

"And Frank had just wanted a son."

That much was true, John knew. Children were all-important to the Westfields. Family was valued above all else. And for a time after Frank and Gloria had first married, Gloria hadn't thought she would be able to give Frank a child. All her attempts to become pregnant had failed. After she and Frank had adopted Tim, however, that had changed. They'd been able to produce three children, all girls. The oldest was seventeen, the youngest thirteen.

"If Tim were to find out, at this point, that his father could be one of several people...John, I just...I don't know what it would do to him and I don't want to find out. Don't you see?" Gloria's expression became fiercely maternal. "I can't risk it. I can't stand idly by and see him set up to be hurt. We've got to do something to stop it."

John agreed, but his reasons were different from his sister-in-law's. They had more to do with protecting his brother's good name, his own campaign, and Tim from the disillusioning truth. His mind focusing on the specifics, he glanced down at the canceled check he still held in his hand. Anger at the possibility Tim was being conned began to build. "Have you talked to this Anne Haynes?"

"No. I wanted to talk to you first. I was afraid if I tried to handle it alone, I'd make things worse, or inadvertently make a political blunder. You know how candidates and their extended families are scrutinized during an election year. If Tim's search uncovered even a hint of scandal, that would be devastating to your campaign. And feeling the way I do right now, I don't trust myself to be able to deal with anyone objectively, least of all the woman who might very well be setting my son up for a broken heart."

"You did the right thing in coming to me," John murmured in approval. Still, the thought of this search of Tim's left him feeling tense and worried, too. What if he couldn't manage to keep the truth of Tim's heritage from his nephew?

"Then you'll take care of it?" Gloria asked, searching his face for the reassurance she so desperately needed.

John nodded slowly, wishing his brother had had more common sense than to adopt a child whose parentage was part of a deliberately hushed scandal.

"And you'll do so without telling Tim what I found out?" Gloria persisted, seeming, for a moment, more like her old self, like the self-assured woman she had been before Frank had died.

John took comfort in seeing Gloria regain some of her former strength. As an uncle, he could only do so much. And that Tim had gotten involved in a possible con was something that should have been addressed first by his parents, not Tim's uncle, standing in for Tim's dad. "Aren't you going to confront him?" he asked.

Looking frantic again, Gloria shook her head, reminding John that even while Frank was alive, she had been loath to tackle problems that came up with the kids. "Not until I know what he's already found out."

Or in other words, John thought, she was leaving all the dirty work to him. Gloria was Tim's parent, not him. Still, she obviously needed help now that Frank wasn't here. "All right," John promised reluctantly, knowing full well it was what Frank would want, "I'll see what I can do."

"Thank you." Gloria closed the distance between them and gave him a quick, sisterly kiss. "I don't know what I'd do without you these days."

John didn't, either, and that troubled him. If Tim ever found out John had been hiding the truth from him, their relationship would be damaged irrevocably. Tim had already lost enough, losing his father so suddenly. They all had.

Lily knocked moments after Gloria had left. "All clear?" she asked, sticking her head in the door.

John grinned and gestured his pretty, energetic assistant inside. "Yep. Sorry about the interruption."

"Your family comes first. I know that," Lily said as she settled herself comfortably in a chair, her stenographer's notebook open on her lap.

His mind was far from the letters they'd been working on. He opened the phone book. Under the white pages was a telephone number and address for Answers, Inc. He scribbled both down on the notepad on his desk, tore off the page and put it into his pocket.

Lily's brows rose in silent inquiry. "Something I should know about?" she asked, taking in the abrupt change of his mood.

John paused. Although Lily had only been with him for three years, ever since she had graduated from the community business college with an associate degree, he knew he could trust the twenty-three-year-old woman implicitly. Besides being a very capable executive assistant, she was also a trusted confidante. She was like a kid sister; she had been with him through the rocky times immediately preceding his divorce, as well as during the current campaign. The only hitch was that sometimes she saw too much of what he was thinking and feeling. However, since she had, he might as well level with her. If he didn't, he'd only pique her insatiable curiosity more. "Tim is doing business with an agency called Answers, Inc.," he said. "Do me a favor and see what you can find out about it. And check out the owner, Anne Haynes, through the local business association and maybe even the district attorney's office."

Lily's mouth tightened speculatively as she scribbled notes. She looked up, the perplexed way she wrinkled her nose making her appear even younger than she was. "You think the business might be an elaborate con of some sort?" she asked.

John frowned. Only his desire to not upset his sister-in-law had kept him from mentioning that possibility. Information about Tim's past was volatile to begin with. In the wrong hands, it would be devastating. "Maybe." John paused, frankly worried. "I don't want Tim hurt."

"I'll keep it quiet," Lily promised, her demeanor serious. She watched as he shrugged into his suit jacket. When his sleeve caught on a cuff link, she got up wordlessly to help him extricate the twisted silk lining from the solid gold square. "Where are you going?"

"Over to check out this agency personally." This Answers, Inc. and Anne Haynes had better be on the level, he thought darkly. Or else.

Chapter Two

"Anne? It's Lei again, in Minneapolis. I'm sorry it's taken me so long, but I finally have that information you wanted about Robert Ryan."

Anne gripped the phone tighter and put the receiver closer to her ear. She had been on pins and needles the entire last week, waiting for word on her birth father from her former client. Now that she was finally about to get it, she didn't know if she was ready. Aware her voice was shaking, she put down the letter she had been proofreading and instructed her young Vietnamese-born friend cautiously, "Go ahead."

"Well, he's a prominent businessman here in Minneapolis. He owns his own paper products company. He's in his early fifties and, judging from the pictures I've seen in the paper, he's not a bad-looking guy, actually. He's something of a society man, attends a lot of charity events and political dinners for the Republican party."

"With his wife?" Anne asked. Was that why Robert Ryan had never returned? Anne was praying he had a very good explanation for the way he'd abandoned them.

"He's not married, but he usually attends those events with a woman."

"The same woman?" That might explain why Robert Ryan hadn't gone back for her mother. He'd been in love with someone else. Like Tim, she realized, she was hanging on to any possible hint of decency her father might possess. To her deep disappointment, Lei couldn't confirm this.

"The pictures I saw from the papers during the past two or three years showed a different woman every time. Usually someone young, beautiful and rich or prominent in some way. He seems to really get around." Lei paused, seeming to realize that something was different about this particular case. "You've really taken a personal interest in this guy, haven't you?"

That was putting it lightly, Anne thought, all the while suppressing the ridiculous, unprecedented urge to shout to the world, "He's my father! And I've found him, at long last!"

For some reason, she couldn't quite bring herself to confide in anyone yet, not even an old friend and former client like Lei. For some reason she was as afraid as she had been when she left Vietnam. After searching for years just to get this far, she was afraid she might jinx things if she jumped the gun and said anything too soon. Robert Ryan had run from her once. She didn't want him running again.

"Did you find out anything more? Was he married at some time in the past? Does he have any kids?"

Lei got back to business. "If he was married, our records don't show it, Anne. Ditto for kids. I have him returning to Minneapolis soon after the war. Of course he wasn't rich and powerful then. He was just a kid, looking for a job and an education."

Remembering the young enlisted man in the photo, Anne could envision that. "Did he get his education?"

"Yeah, an undergraduate degree in marketing, with a minor in business, and then an MBA. All told, it took him almost seven years. He was working for a manufacturing firm full-time and going to school nights. At first, he attended community college and then the University of Minneapolis, on the G.I. bill."

"Anything else?" Anne asked, aware her heart was racing and her hands were perspiring. In her head, there was a picture of Robert Ryan as he had been years ago—impossibly young, handsome, with incredibly kind eyes. Eyes that had lied when he'd told her mother he was coming back...

"Sorry," Lei said, "that's about it."

Briefly, disappointment colored her mood. She knew it was unrealistic of her, but she had been hoping for some laudable explanation of what had happened. Instead, all she had found out, besides the fact that her natural father was alive and well, was that he had gone on to build a nice life without her or her mother. And apparently he'd done so with no regrets.

But, Anne realized, that wasn't Lei's fault and she couldn't take her disappointment out on her friend.

"What do I owe you for your time on the phone and at the library?" Anne asked, making her voice as cheerful as possible. Had she her druthers, she would have gone to Minnesota personally, but she didn't have the money. And she was spending every spare moment on the Tim Westfield case.

"Nothing," Lei said firmly. "Consider this on the house, for helping me locate my half sister two years ago."

"How is Mai?" Anne asked, thinking of the two Vietnamese sisters who had been orphaned during the war and subsequently adopted by different families. Mai had been in California, Lei in Minnesota. A year ago, Anne had helped reunite them.

"She's great," Lei confided. "Better now that we have each other. Our adoptive families even got together around Christmastime. We met in Vail, for a skiing holiday." Her voice choked up suddenly. "It was really great. Seeing her again, I felt like I finally *belonged*, that I'd come home. You know what I mean?"

No, she didn't. But not about to rain on Lei's hard-won parade, Anne forced cheer into her voice and said, "I'm happy for you." And she was.

"I know. And I owe you a lot," Lei spoke with a happy musical lilt in her voice. "That's why this one is on me."

Wishing she could see Lei in person and give her a hug for her generosity of spirit, Anne accepted the gift with the sincerity in which it was given. "You'll stop in and see me if you ever come to Concord?"

"I promise," Lei said, "and in the meantime, maybe you could help another friend of mine." Briefly Lei told Anne about her friend, Trong.

"Sure, I'll see him," Anne finally promised, realizing once again that there was no shortage of people needing help, and no greater satisfaction than when she was able to give it.

"I knew you wouldn't let me down," Lei said. After they hung up, Anne went back to a letter, finished proofreading it, and folded it into thirds. She was just stuffing it into an envelope addressed to the department of immigration when the doorbell rang. Hoping it was the postman with some good news, she got up.

It wasn't the postman. She'd never met him before in her life. But she knew who he was. She was willing to bet everyone in New Hampshire old enough to read the newspapers or turn on the television news did. She felt a little star-struck. She'd never been this close to such a famous politician, never mind such a ruggedly good-looking one. She stared up at him. She knew from the news that he was single again. After several years, she couldn't imagine why. Surely women were lined up around the block to go out with him. Handsome, rich, ambitious, smart, gregarious to the core—what was there not to like?

"Ms. Haynes, I presume?" John Westfield said grimly.

John had expected someone older, sleazier. Instead, he found himself facing a beautiful woman in her late twenties. Of Amerasian descent, she radiated a vitality and warmth he found even more disconcerting than the directness of her dark blue eyes. There was something so innocent about her, so pure, so at odds with her contemptible profession.

"Yes," Anne affirmed her identity, the accusatory note in his low baritone bringing her promptly back to reality and to the danger inherent in this situation. When Tim had first come to her, she had been afraid that his powerful family would somehow find out and come down on *her*. The week without such ramifications that had passed had given her a sense of security she now knew was false. Sensing that any show of nervousness on her part would be interpreted as guilt, she gathered her composure around her like an invisible shield and nodded at her visitor regally. "Mr. Westfield. How nice of you to drop by."

"I see you know who I am," he said.

Knowing how the Westfields tended to close ranks when threatened, Anne felt a tiny shiver run down her spine. She did not want to be at odds, either publicly or privately, with a powerful man like John Westfield.

"Who in this city doesn't know who you are?" she returned lightly. Her nerves were tightening more with every second and she was painfully aware of everything about him, from his large, quarterback's build, to his polished wing-tip shoes. His suit was dark blue and expensive, his blue-and-white-striped shirt starched, but his deep burgundy tie was slightly askew. She liked the lack of male vanity that implied. He was clearly a man who cared more about substance than appearance. She also liked the slightly rough-hewn features of his face—the thick shelflike brows, the broad nose, the wide mouth and delectably full lips, the golden complexion and his strong chin; his hair was a glossy medium brown, cut short and neat. She didn't like the way he was looking at her, as if she was a shyster out to take advantage. But she also knew she wasn't likely to get rid of him without at least talking to him, not when he was obviously this concerned about his nephew.

"Would you like to come in?" She opened the front door a little wider, acutely aware of the cluttered office space behind her. Her house was small and ancient. Upstairs was her bedroom and bath. Downstairs was her living room "office," and the kitchen and the mudroom, which held her washer and dryer. Apart from the tiny detached garage out back, that was it.

John Westfield hesitated. The last thing he wanted to do was fraternize with the enemy. On the other hand, this was no conversation to have on her doorstep. "All right," he said finally.

She led the way, motioning to the ancient sofa she'd bought at a garage sale and slipcovered in a bright floral print. "Can I get you some coffee or perhaps iced tea?"

"No. Thanks." Aware his voice was still too abrupt, his demeanor bordering on rudeness, John paused and then, very reluctantly, sat down.

Wanting this interview to be informal and friendly, Anne eschewed the chair behind her desk and took a seat in the armchair next to him. Aware his thorough glance had taken in every inch of her tall, slender frame, she tugged her short peach-colored skirt down as far as it would go. "How may I help you, Mr. Westfield?" she asked. There was no sense in giving away what he didn't already know. Tim had wanted this to be kept quiet.

"Let's cut the crap, shall we?" John Westfield seemed to remain seated with considerable effort. His jaw tightened and his eyes honed in on her face. He detested people who took advantage of others for their own gain. "I know my nephew Tim has been here, that he's given you money."

Anne's shoulders stiffened. "Did Tim tell you this?" she bit out.

John sighed. "I don't think it matters how I found out—"

"It does to me." She stood and appraised him, her glance hostile.

He stood, too, continuing as if she hadn't spoken, his voice a dangerous purr. "The point is I know. And so does his mother."

He stepped closer, the woodsy scent of his aftershave assaulting her senses. Seeing the uneasiness on his face, she felt her throat go dry and tight. Her gut instinct told her he was hiding something. Something he didn't want either Tim or her to know. He was getting under her skin in a way no one ever had before. "What did Tim say?" As she narrowed her eyes at him, her pulse did a rapid staccato.

John frowned and looked away.

"I haven't spoken to him."

Again, she saw his evasion and wondered at it. On television, at least, he came across as such a forthright, direct man. "Why not?" Why was he afraid to confront his nephew but not afraid to confront her? John didn't seem the type to shy away from conflict.

He looked at her. She was near enough to see the green fire in his eyes and his anguish. The man was a reluctant participant here, Anne realized. And he knew more about Tim than he was willing to share.

"I didn't want to upset him," John finally muttered.

"But you don't mind upsetting me?" He had marched in here, his judgment about her made before he ever set foot in the door and she hated that!

He pinned her with a searing look, unwilling to ease up in the slightest. "You seem to be able to take care of yourself," he commented boldly.

"So can Tim," she snapped back. No wonder Tim was frustrated; his family was treating him like a mindless imbecile.

Without warning, pleading filled his eyes. "He's vulnerable right now, dammit. His father just died."

"I know that," Anne said softly.

Surprise flickered across his face at the compassion in her voice. Silence stretched between them. He was less tense now.

Realizing the loss was mutual, that John was hurting from Frank Westfield's death, too, she offered her condolences in a more subdued, penitent tone. "I'm sorry." He had been through a rough time. She wasn't making it any easier on him.

He studied her, trying to see if her sympathy was genuine. His expression softened and for a moment their visual exchange was without rancor. "Thanks."

Silence fell again, more awkwardly this time. "Tim seems like a nice boy," Anne said.

"He is." John rested his hands on his hips, pushing the edges of his suit coat back, to reveal the taut trim lines of his stomach and the sinewy silhouette of his upper chest. He looked away from her full, soft lips and golden skin. This would be so much easier if he could just level with her. But he couldn't, not without risking his relationship with his nephew and his campaign. "Look," he said gruffly. "I want you to stop working for Tim. Now."

He obviously expected her to cave in to his demands. She didn't know whether to be amused or annoyed. "That isn't up to you to decide," she pointed out with forced casualness.

His temper flared once again. "The hell it's not."

"This is Tim's decision."

"Tim isn't thinking straight right now."

"I think he is, and it's his life."

Knowing they'd reached a stalemate, they stared at each other. His incredibly light green eyes clouded over.

The more she studied him, the more he withdrew.

Finally he took another approach, one, no doubt, Anne thought wryly, he figured was sure to appeal to her feminine heart. "Surely you can understand. This is hurting his mother tremendously."

She knew that was true; all adoptive mothers suffered pangs when their adopted children searched out their natural parents. But there had to be more to John's desire to silence her than just his sister-in-law's hurt feelings. He was too desperate and driven. "And perhaps it might hurt your campaign?" Anne folded her arms at her waist, her expression as smug and deftly insinuating as his had been earlier. "After all, why remind the potential voters you have an adopted relative with some foreign 'gook' blood? Right?"

That hit home. She saw instantly, from his affronted reaction, she had been wrong. He wasn't ashamed of Tim's lineage.

"That's a hell of a thing to say," he shot back fiercely, "especially from someone who damn well ought to know better! I don't care what color his skin is or where his parents came from! I love my nephew." With satisfaction, he watched the guilty color creep into her cheeks. "Not that it matters to me what you think.

"I want voters to vote for me because they believe in me, not because of who may or may not be in my family tree. And I want you to leave my nephew and my family the hell alone."

His fierce protectiveness of his family was something she admired. Nevertheless, she couldn't, wouldn't give in. "It's not that simple." His glare turned challenging and it took all her courage to speak evenly. "You didn't hire me."

"Maybe not," he countered smoothly, "but I can bring an investigation down on you." He leaned closer, until their noses were a scant inch and a half apart. "I can have every law enforcement branch in this state scrutinizing your business methods with a fine-tooth comb." He didn't doubt they'd find something amiss.

Her chin lifted higher, but inside she was quaking. Many of the things she did were, if not borderline illegal, at least downright unethical and under the table. She didn't want it that way, but sometimes that was the only way she could proceed. It was impossible to get anything from certain countries without offering bribes. But that wasn't something either John Westfield or their own state department would condone.

"You'd do that to your nephew?" she asked softly, making no effort to mask her frustration, hoping he was bluffing.

John Westfield studied her, weighing his options and the risks. As much as he wanted to expose Anne Haynes for the fraud she was, he couldn't do so without also exposing Tim to equal scrutiny. And that was a risk he couldn't take.

"What would it take to get you to drop this?" he asked heavily at last, his eyes still on hers.

"Tim, asking me to do so," she answered simply, aware that with his nearness her heart had started a slow, heavy beat.

Again she had the sensation he was withholding ten times more than he was saying. Was it possible he already knew something about his nephew's roots? Something he wanted kept covered up?

In the background, the phone rang. Anne excused herself. She listened, murmured, "One moment please," and handed the receiver over to John. "It's your assistant, at campaign headquarters."

With a look of concern and a murmured thanks, he took the receiver from her hands. "Lily, hi. What's up?" He turned his back to Anne.

From the rear, his shoulders looked even more powerful. She wondered just how many and which sports he had played in his youth and what sports he still played. He had the physique of a man who was very active and planned to stay that way.

John sighed and buried his face in his open palm. He shook his head sadly, still either taking the bad news in or listening to his assistant. Finally he said, "Okay. Tell them I'll be right over. Yeah, have the press meet me there. I want to put as much pressure on as possible. I want people to see what they've done." He hung up the phone.

"The bill that would've provided housing for the homeless was just defeated in the state senate," John explained, looking very disappointed and a little harried. "I'm due over at the public housing project in the Heights to talk to the people there. I want to reassure them that this doesn't mean we're going to give up the fight to provide decent, affordable housing for the indigent in our state." He compressed his lips, looking both anxious to leave and at the same time reluctant to walk away from his meeting with Anne. She knew how he felt. She wanted this little tête-à-tête to end... and she didn't. There was still too much unresolved and too much he was hiding.

His gaze scanned her slender form and he cleared his throat. "We still need to talk, Ms. Haynes."

He wanted to change her mind. And although she knew he would never be able to do that, there was a small part of her that wanted to see him try, if only to see what else he might inadvertently reveal in the process.

"How about riding over with me to the Heights?" he continued. "We'd have a good fifteen minutes to talk on the way there, another fifteen minutes on the way back." He regarded her patiently, his expression pragmatic. "What do you say?"

Whether John realized it or not, Tim needed his uncle on his side, every bit as much as she needed for John not to actively work against her. Maybe, if she talked to him some more she could at least convince him that she wasn't a crook. "Okay," she said, grabbing her purse and her keys. If it wasn't just concern for his own political campaign that made him ask her to stop her search, then what was it? What deep, dark family secret was John trying to hide?

Chapter Three

"I don't understand why you don't want Tim to find his natural parents," Anne said, once they were en route to the housing project. Reaching up, she untwisted the seat belt, which had tangled just above her breasts. "You obviously care about him a great deal."

"Yes, I do," John said firmly, one hand grasping the steering wheel of his shiny black BMW sedan, the other resting on the soft gray leather armrest between them. For some reason, Anne couldn't take her eyes from that hand. The fingers were long and strong looking; it was a capable hand that was no stranger to work. "Which is why I don't want to see him hurt," John continued straightforwardly.

Anne forced her eyes back to the scenery whizzing by. "And you think finding his natural parents will do that," she ascertained dryly. Curious, she turned to face him.

Keeping his eyes on the road, he shifted uncomfortably behind the wheel, the strong muscles in his thigh flexing as he moved his foot smoothly from accelerator to brake, and then back again.

"Tim has this fairy-tale idea of what he thinks is going to happen when he finds his natural parents, that somehow his finding them is going to make everything all right. It'll make up for the fact that he was born into unfortunate circumstances, abandoned, and then adopted." John shrugged. "I don't buy it. I think given the circumstances and the amount of time that has passed, that Tim's presence in his natural parents' lives couldn't be anything but an intrusion. Providing of course he can find them." John slanted her a warning glance. "And I'm not certain that he can, even with your... help."

The way he said "help" made her sound more foe than friend to his nephew. Needing some air, Anne rolled down her window an inch. The fresh spring breeze cooled her overheated features but did nothing to ease the increasing constriction around her heart. "You think I'm a con artist, don't you?" It wasn't the first time she'd ever been accused of being less than honest. That John thought of her in that way hurt more than she had expected it would.

John slowed the car as they approached a stoplight. After they had stopped, he eased his right arm along the back of the front seat and turned to look at her. "On the surface, you don't look like one, but then, most successful ones don't. That's what makes them so good."

"You speak as if you've had experience with cons."

Briefly bitterness shone in his light green eyes. John turned his glance from the soft, silky length of her black hair. "All the Westfields have." He released a long, weary breath as painful memories surfaced. They had never expected betrayal, yet it had happened. His grandmother's former social secretary had written a sensational exposé, painfully detailing the most intimate details of their family life. One of his cousins had been the embarrassed subject of a kiss-and-tell book, written by a former lover. And there had been a number of unauthorized biographies and made-for-television movies on the extended family. The Westfields had learned not to trust outsiders or take anyone at face value.

He turned to Anne again, wanting her to know he saw through her, too. "There's always someone trying to benefit at my family's expense."

"Has anyone succeeded?" she asked lightly, her curiosity about John Westfield and his powerful family undaunted. How much of what was reported about them was true and how much was not?

"Succeeded? I guess that's a matter of definition. If you mean, has anyone made a buck off us, the answer is yes. But as for conning us, no, not yet."

She detected a warning in his low tone. But she had no intention of taking Tim or anyone in his family to the cleaners. John would realize that and grow to trust her. They all would. Used to proving herself, she had no problem doing it one more time.

Traffic continued to be heavy and John didn't speak again until they had reached the public housing project in the Heights. He parked on the cracked, uneven blacktop, his shiny new BMW looking oddly out of place next to the battered cars in the lot. He turned off the ignition and released his seat belt. Sliding his right arm along the back of the seat once again, he turned to face her. "I don't suppose there's any talking you out of helping Tim," he remarked.

First bribery, then charm, Anne thought, taking in his pleading, "let's be reasonable" smile. The man didn't know when to quit. "No," she said softly, "there isn't." As gregarious as John was, she sensed that it was unusual for him to come on so strongly with someone he barely knew. He seemed more straightforward than that. "What else is going on, John?" she asked warily. What did he fear was going to happen? If she was in the middle of something unsavory or even dangerous, she had the right to know so.

Tense seconds ticked by. Evidently he realized she wasn't giving up and that his only chance to enlist her aid was to level with her. "This is off the record," he said shortly.

Anne tried to contain her excitement. "Okay."

"Not for publication of any sort," he warned.

She shrugged and spread her hands. "Okay."

"Since my brother died, there have been a lot of problems at home." John chose his words carefully. "My sister-in-law, Gloria, is a very loving woman, but she's also very fragile. She's had a hard time dealing with Frank's death, and so have all their kids. They're acting out their grief in a variety of ways." He frowned. "Tim, in particular, has been giving her a hard time, exerting his independence."

"All kids at eighteen do that," Anne reminded John, hearing the censure in his voice.

A weary look on his face, John rubbed the back of his neck. "Yeah, but Gloria doesn't need to be dealing with that right now," he disagreed.

"Have you talked to Tim?"

John nodded curtly. "Not about this yet, but about other things. He thinks no one in the family understands him."

And maybe that was true, Anne thought, at least when it came to discovering his roots. No one in her family understood her need to do the same.

"He's got this crazy notion that because he's adopted he doesn't belong," John continued emotionally.

"And you think he does?"

Again, John looked shocked. "Hell, yes, he's a Westfield through and through. He just hasn't realized it yet."

Anne warmed to the underlying affection she heard in John's voice, even as she railed against his overprotectiveness. "Maybe searching for his past will help him discover that," she pointed out reasonably.

John remained unconvinced. He faced her stubbornly. "And maybe it will just confuse him even more," he countered in a soft, troubled voice.

Again, John's worry seemed to go far beyond what they were discussing. "He has a right to know about his past," she insisted. "Everyone does."

John's head lifted. "Even if it hurts a lot of innocent people?"

Anne swallowed, but the reflexive action did little to lubricate her parched throat. "Tim didn't create the situation that landed him in America," she countered. "Others did. If it hurts those people—"

"And whatever families or lives they've created for themselves now—"

"So be it."

He studied her in mute disagreement. "You really believe that, don't you?" he asked sardonically.

Anne nodded firmly. "Yes. And you don't." And that didn't make sense. John seemed like such a fair person, from what she knew of him politically. He seemed open to people and ideas. But maybe that was just an image he wanted to cultivate on television, she thought. Maybe what she saw there wasn't really John at all. Maybe in reality he was selfish and self-centered, concerned mainly about his own political career. Maybe he just didn't want to deal with Tim and Gloria's emotional crisis. And maybe he already knew more than all three of them put together. There had to be some reason he was so convinced this search of hers would come to a bad end.

John had never met so tenacious a woman. His gut twisting, he stared at the run-down buildings in front of them. He had to find a way to get her to back off. His nephew's future depended on it.

"I think Tim has all the family, all the roots, all the past he will ever need right here in Concord," he said finally.

Across the lot, a news truck pulled up and parked. A camera crew, loaded down with video equipment, got out. "Why not give him a chance to discover that for himself, then?" Anne asked impatiently, knowing their time to talk was running out. "Hasn't it occurred to you that Tim's search into the past might help him better accept and appreciate the present?"

Ignoring her question, he glanced at his watch pointedly, and then at the members of the crew, who were waving hello to him. Anne watched John smile and wave back. When he spoke to her again, his voice was dismissive. "We'd better get going. I'm supposed to say a few words over in the manager's office."

Quite a crowd had gathered by the time they joined the others. Because there were too many people to fit into the tiny manager's office, the gathering of resident families, homeless people, reporters, and political aides was held outdoors in the bright May sunshine.

"Now what are we going to do, Mr. Westfield?" a large black woman with a baby on her hip demanded. "I gotta have a place to live."

"Yeah," the woman beside her said, "I've been on the waiting list for a place a long time, too. New apartments would have taken care of that."

John held up a hand to stop the flow of impassioned protests. "We haven't given up. If we don't get the money from the state or the federal government, then we'll go to the private sector, but one way or another we'll manage something before another winter sets in. I promise."

Listening to him, Anne decided he was a politician, all right. He deftly evaded and covered up when dealing with her and Tim, and then spoke honestly and compassionately to the poor.

"What about repairs to the apartments?" a Heights resident asked. "My plumbing hasn't worked right in three years."

"Yeah, and this place hasn't been painted in years!" a second resident chimed in.

"We deserve better than we're getting, for the rent we're paying!" a third tenant declared hotly.

"And what about a playground? Our kids need someplace to play in the spring and summer!"

John listened patiently to all the complaints, making notes occasionally and talking realistically to the residents about what could be done and what couldn't. They could add more units in the two vacant fields behind the projects and manage the necessary repairs. Things like repainting the outside of the projects and finding money for a playground would have to come later.

No one liked the idea of waiting, but everyone was able to see how passionately John wanted to help. Watching him, Anne was struck by his generosity. Why couldn't he be equally empathetic, honest and open with his nephew? What was he hiding? What did he know?

"Sorry that took so long," John said later as he walked her back to his car.

"It's okay. It was important," Anne said. She cast a glance at the vacant fields that stood behind the buildings. "Do you really think you'll be able to do something about building more units before winter?" she asked skeptically.

"I know I will," John said confidently, pausing as they reached his car. "Why?"

Anne stepped back slightly, letting the cool spring breeze stir her hair. "Well, you have the election coming up." Not to mention his problems with his family.

"That won't stop me from lobbying for funding for public housing. In fact it will give me even more opportunity to do so." His eyes narrowed thoughtfully as he scanned her face. "You don't believe me, do you?"

Anne shrugged. "I just think you promised more than one man should realistically be expected to deliver. The wheels of bureaucracy grind slowly and all that."

John opened the rear door to his car and shrugged out of his jacket. Folding it carelessly, he tossed it in the back. "Or in other words, you think I'm full of hot air."

At her tactful silence, he sighed and said, green eyes glinting, "I'll prove it to you, then."

Both surprised and amused by the way he had taken up the challenge, she raised a brow. "How?"

He slammed the back door, but delayed opening hers. "There's a black-tie dinner tomorrow night. It's being given to raise money for my fall campaign, but I'll use it to lobby for public housing."

She watched him loosen his tie and undo the top button on his shirt. "You could be costing yourself donations, you know, if you're successful."

He shrugged, unconcerned. He unfastened his cuff links and rolled up his shirtsleeves. He faced her. "It'll be for a worthy cause. So, what do you say?"

Anne was quiet. Why would a man with John's obvious compassion not be more inclined to simply give Tim what he wanted, especially now that Frank, Tim's father, was dead? Why was he so open and straightforward with the people, and so secretive and mysterious with her? It was almost as if he were afraid of what would happen if Tim did find his parents, with Anne's help. But the fear wasn't only for himself or his own political career; it was for Tim and his sister-in-law, Gloria. For the entire Westfield family.

"What else is going on, John?" she asked. She didn't like games and she liked cover-ups even less.

"What do you mean?"

"What are you so afraid of?"

"Nothing," he denied hotly.

"Like hell." Anne studied him bluntly. "You know something, don't you? Something about Tim's past—"

"You're talking nonsense. The adoption was strictly confidential. That went both ways—"

"Then why are you so nervous? What do you think's going to happen? That he'll find biological parents he's ashamed of or get blackmailed or find out the adoption was illegal and he's not really an American citizen at all? What?"

"You have quite an imagination." It wasn't a compliment.

"And you're not as adept at this cover-up business as you'd like," Anne volleyed back, her eyes holding his determinedly.

Anne Haynes was a pain in the neck and one hell of an adversary. More than ever, John needed to find a way to discourage her. He remembered his father's advice: Know thy enemy. "So," he said wryly, "Back to the fund-raiser. Was that a yes or a no?"

Her chin lifted another notch. Her midnight-blue eyes radiated disbelief. "Knowing what I think of you... you still want me to go?" she asked in a low, incredulous tone.

I've got to keep an eye on you somehow. "Yes."

"Why?"

"Why not? You seem like a concerned citizen. You're bright, vigilant and judging from the look on your face when I spoke to the group, compassionate... exactly the type of person we need to help find homes for the less fortunate."

"So," she concluded wryly, "you're trying to recruit me." She wasn't going to let him distract her from her real mission, helping Tim find his Korean family.

"There's a little more to it than that. For Tim's sake, I'd like to get to know you better." He also wanted her on his side, but he had no idea in hell how he was going to manage that.

Anne couldn't deny she was curious about him, too. She wanted to solve the mystery behind his behavior.

"I'll go," she said, "but only on the condition you not bring up the subject of my helping Tim."

He sighed. "Agreed. For tomorrow night only, though." He lifted a warning finger and pointed it her way. "After that, all bets are off."

"You won't change my mind," Anne cautioned.

"That," John said, with the resolute complacence of a man well used to getting what he wanted, "remains to be seen."

"How did the meeting at the Heights go?" Lily asked. She was at his side with an icy glass of lemonade and a small package of honey-roasted peanuts.

John took both, and settled back in his chair. He had never asked Lily to wait on him hand and foot. He had tried to tell her that early on, when she had first started working for him, but she had insisted rather passionately that she didn't mind, and in fact, prided herself on her ability to anticipate his needs. He had to admit that she was a damn good executive assistant. She was able to work quickly and efficiently, never complained about the long hours and was always willing to be there as a friend.

"The meeting was tough, actually," John finally said. "I tried to reassure the people as best I could but I don't think they really believed me."

"They'll believe you when you deliver on your promises," Lily said.

John wished he had Lily's unflagging confidence in his ability to work miracles. He also wished Anne Haynes hadn't doubted him so openly.

"How was the meeting with Ms. Haynes?"

That, John thought, was much harder to qualify. "Less productive, I'm afraid."

"Is she a con artist?" Kicking off her shoes, Lily curled up on the sofa.

"I don't know," he said. He wanted to trust Anne, but his family had been burned too many times in the past for him to do so. They were wealthy. They were powerful. And because they were all in public life, they were easy marks. Finishing the last of his peanuts, he crumpled the foil bag and tossed it into the trash. "What did you find out?"

"The agency is eight years old. There have been no reports to the Better Business Bureau or the local district attorney or the state Attorney General's office about the possibility of fraud. Which doesn't mean, of course, Anne Haynes hasn't done anything wrong, or taken anyone's money for no reason, only that no one has complained about it. What did you think of the lady personally?"

Well, John thought, he hadn't expected her to be so young or so pretty. When she'd opened the door to her small, cluttered house he'd been rendered speechless, able only to take in the thick fall of silky black shoulder-length hair and the fringe of bangs that framed her heart-shaped face. Hers was an exotic beauty, enhanced by the glow of her golden skin, her soft full lips, and dark blue eyes. Before even two minutes had passed, he had memorized every inch of her slender, willowy frame. She was feminine, but there was nothing fragile about her. Anne Haynes was strong-willed and quick tempered. She could stand up for herself and others, like Tim. He admired her, but dreaded dealing with her on a continuing adversarial level.

Lily slanted him a curious look as if wondering where he had drifted off to. Remembering he had yet to answer his assistant's question about what he thought of Anne personally, John said gruffly, "She seems on the level."

"And?" Lily prompted impatiently, as if resenting his uncharacteristic silence.

John shrugged. "And... nothing," he said evasively. "She rode over to the Heights with me because we weren't done talking." At Lily's surprised look, he added, "I was hoping to talk her out of helping Tim en route."

Lily arched a brow. "And did you?"

"No. But I'm not through yet, either." Anne Haynes had gotten to him the way no woman ever had. She'd made him look at himself and his actions with microscopic intensity. He admitted grudgingly, "I'm taking her to that black-tie dinner tomorrow night."

Lily's mouth dropped open. She leaned forward apprehensively. "Do you really think that's wise?"

"If she's a fraud, I'm going to expose her."

Lily looked genuinely distressed. "And if she's not? What then, John?"

His assistant didn't have to point out to him how dangerous it could be to get involved, even marginally, with the wrong woman at this crucial stage of his campaign. Still, his family came first. And he'd made a promise to Gloria and to Frank. "If she's not," he said resolutely, looking out the window at the Governor's mansion down the street, "then I'm going to find a way to get her on my side. To persuade her not to help Tim."

"Because of the campaign." Lily clucked sympathetically.

John let Lily's misconception pass without comment. His reasons had nothing to do with the campaign and everything to do with his family. It would be simpler if he could just tell Anne and Tim why he didn't want Tim to search for his roots... if he could tell them he and Frank had already known who Tim's parents were and why they'd had to give him up for adoption. Normally honest and forthright, it was extremely difficult for John to pretend he knew nothing. He hated secrets. He hated keeping Tim in the dark.

But he couldn't tell the truth without betraying his brother. He had promised Frank no one would ever know or be able to hurt Tim with the suppressed scandal that had surrounded his birth. It was a promise John intended to keep. Otherwise, Tim's world would be blown apart. His relationship with John would be shot all to hell, too. Because like it or not, John had been a part of the cover-up from day one.

Yes, his nephew would be hurt and disappointed if he never found out who his natural parents were. But those feelings of frustration would pass, and in the end he would be much better off. John had only to convince Anne Haynes of that, too. Anne—with the silky black hair, exotic good looks, and midnight-blue eyes. Anne—with the steely determination, natural skepticism and ready compassion. John would convince her no matter what it took.

Chapter Four

"You're up bright and early."

"So are you." Anne faced her breezy older sister Leslie across the threshold at eight the following morning. Leslie was right. Anne usually didn't climb out of bed until seven-thirty, but this morning she had showered, dressed and read the morning paper before seven, and she had made her airline reservations for Minneapolis by eight.

"What brings you by so early?" Anne picked up the slip of paper that had her flight number and airline on it and slid it into her pocket. It wasn't like Leslie to just pop in, unannounced. Usually she was too busy with her free-lance work as a tax accountant and her duties as president of the local PTA to do anything not on her or her family's schedule.

Leslie shrugged. "We haven't heard much from you lately. I wanted to know if you wanted to have dinner with me and Ted and the kids tonight."

Anne knew she hadn't been keeping up family relations, but she felt torn. Part of her wanted to tell them she had finally located Robert Ryan. The other part of her didn't want to hurt them. If they found out she had still been searching all this time, they would wonder why they weren't enough for her. Now that she had plans to visit her natural father the following week, the situation was intensified.

Nevertheless, it was good to see Leslie. Anne realized how much she had missed seeing her, even if most of the time the two of them didn't have a whole lot in common. "Thanks for thinking of me, sis, but... I can't. Not tonight."

"Oh?" Leslie arched a curious brow and helped herself to a cup of coffee. She pushed her chestnut curls in place and fastened her gray eyes on Anne's face. "Got a date?"

Anne hedged. "Not exactly." Because they were thirteen years apart in age, Anne had never gotten in the habit of confiding any more about her romantic life to Leslie than she did to her mother. With more than usual care, Anne spread butter and jam on an English muffin and announced as blandly as possible, "I'm going to a political fund-raiser tonight for John Westfield."

"Wow!" Leslie breathed. "Who's your date?"

"John Westfield."

Leslie whistled. "How in the world did you manage *that*?"

Anne blushed despite herself. Though John seemed nice, he was definitely withholding something shady. Besides that, he clearly suspected she was a fraud, although why he'd think that when she'd had so many successful cases, she didn't know. "It's no big deal, really, and we're just going as acquaintances."

Leslie gave her a look that said "sure you are." "Where'd you meet?" Her expression was suddenly as bland as Anne's.

"Through work. It's a long story."

Leslie looked thoughtful, but didn't press. "Did you know that dinner is a thousand dollars a plate?"

Anne stared glumly at the paper's society page, her mood falling fast. "I just found out." What had she been thinking when she accepted John's invitation? She would never fit in there. She knew it. And this latest twist only added to her misery. Try as she might, she couldn't hide her anxiety.

"What are you going to wear?" Leslie asked.

"I don't know." Anne emitted a troubled sigh, happy this once to be leaning on her capable older sister for moral support. "I don't have anything nearly sophisticated enough."

"Neither do I or I'd lend it to you." Leslie paused and set down her coffee cup. She looked down at her own figure, which was pleasantly rounded after the births of her two children. "Not that it'd fit, anyway," she remarked with a good-natured laugh. She continued seriously, "I don't suppose your budget could take buying something at McQuade's or She?"

"No," Anne shook her head sadly at her sister's mention of Concord's most elegant dress shops. Not if she wanted to make this month's mortgage on her house.

"Well, there's a dress shop downtown that specializes in used dresses. Cast-offs from society ladies. It's run by the ladies' auxiliary."

An hour later, Anne was in a dressing room, trying on a navy chiffon gown, with a plunging neckline and handkerchief hem. "It's too dark," she said, thinking it gave her skin an unattractive bluish cast.

Leslie nodded at the plunging neckline. "And too low."

Next was an emerald gown of velvet brocade. Anne studied herself critically in the mirror. "It ages me."

Leslie disagreed. She thought it just made Anne look mature. She handed Anne the next gown anyway, a vibrant teal-blue taffeta with a full ruffled skirt. "Too young," Anne said, dismissing it with a disgruntled shake of her head. "I look like a senior going to the prom."

Ten dresses later, her patience exhausted, Leslie threw up her hands in exasperation. "You know what your problem is?" she chided affectionately. "You're worrying too much about fitting in there tonight. They're just people, you know. They put on their pants, same as you and me, one leg at a time. You have nothing to fear, Anne. I don't care who your date is or where you're going."

"That's easy for you to say. You always did fit in. You never had to work at it like I did." Looking at the devastation on Leslie's face, Anne wished she could take her foolish words back.

Leslie sat down on the chair in the corner, a mixture of guilt and regret in her expression. At that moment, she looked every one of her forty-one years. "I'm sorry, Anne. I didn't mean to patronize you," she said softly.

"I know. I know you were trying to help."

"It was hard on you, wasn't it," Leslie whispered sympathetically, "coming to this country?"

Anne put aside her regrets, and her thoughts of how everything had been foreign and strange to her then, from the food she ate at meals to the shoes she put on her feet and the bed she slept in at night. "I'm okay," she reassured her older sister firmly.

That was all behind her now. And once she met Robert Ryan, a feat she had vowed to manage by July 4, no matter what, it would be over for good. Her American father would tell her why he had never come back to her and her mother. Secure in the knowledge of the past and the reasons for it, secure in her heritage, she would at last be a real American. She would finally be able to make peace with her past and go on.

Again, Leslie searched her face, wanting so badly to help. "You're sure?"

Anne nodded. "Yes." She reached for a dress on the hook next to the door, the eighth one she'd tried. "I'll take this one," she decided. Leslie was right. She was being silly and overcritical. Picking out a dress was easy, especially when compared to the trial by fire she would face tonight.

"I HAD A FEELING you'd be on time," John remarked as Anne locked the door behind her.

"You're the guest of honor," Anne remarked, trying very hard to keep her voice neutral and not betray the continuing suspicion she felt toward him. "I knew you couldn't afford to be late."

"Meaning what? If I hadn't been, you would have kept me waiting?" he teased.

She cast him a wry glance, all too aware of how handsome he looked in his black tuxedo and crisp white shirt. His chestnut-brown hair had been combed with exceptional care. After-shave clung to his closely shaven jaw. As attractive as John was, she couldn't shake the persistent feeling he was trying to throw her off her guard. Or worse, seduce her off the case with his world of money and glamour. She knew what he didn't, however, that nothing and no one got in her way when she was trying to help someone. Her inner determination doubled when it came to someone as young and vulnerable as Tim Westfield.

She shrugged her shoulders elegantly and picked up the threads of their repartee. "Sorry to disappoint you, I'm one of those women who is always on time."

His light green eyes glimmered with humor. "Not a bad trait to have," he remarked gallantly, slipping a steadying hand beneath her elbow as they moved down her front steps. "I could get used to that."

He dropped his hand as soon as they reached the walk, yet Anne remained breathlessly aware of his touch all the way to his car. "Who's going to be there tonight?"

His gaze roved her slender figure, taking in the clinging slim floor-length white jersey dress with the beaded bodice, jewel neckline and low V-shaped back. "A lot of people," he replied, the approval in his eyes making her warm all over. "The mayor, a couple of senators, friends of the family, wealthy contributors, the usual mix. I'll introduce you around."

If he noticed her nervousness, he didn't show it. Nor did he seem to realize how thoroughly she planned to observe the Westfields, one and all. They were keeping something from both Tim and her.

"Thanks." Anne forced a smile as she adjusted the posts of her gold earrings. Intuition told her tonight would be very informative. She couldn't wait to get started.

Fortunately John was as good as his word. No sooner had they walked into the banquet hall than he was introducing her to his sister-in-law, Gloria Westfield. "Hello, Anne," Gloria said graciously, motioning Anne to a seat at her table. John moved off to say hello to others. "I'm glad you could come. John and I both are."

Her movements deceptively casual, Anne dropped into a chair and placed her shimmery gold evening bag on her lap. She disliked prying into the intimate lives of others. No matter how nobly motivated her actions, it always made her feel as if she were intruding unfairly. Yet the Westfields had left her no choice.

She studied Tim's mother and was unnerved to see how fragile Gloria looked. Anne didn't want to make the recent widow's situation any worse. She could tell just by looking at Gloria that the already-slender woman had lost weight she could ill afford to lose.

There were bluish circles of fatigue under her eyes that makeup couldn't hide and a suppressed pain and fear in her face that seemed to go soul-deep. "You talked to John about me?" Anne asked.

"Yes, I did," Gloria affirmed honestly, her hands beginning to tremble, "at great length. We're both very concerned about my son, Tim."

To Anne's surprise, Gloria didn't seem secretive, not the way John did. She was just a concerned mother; that was all.

Still, Tim was not only her client, but a young man of legal age. Both she and Tim deserved not only the Westfields' respect, but the right to do as they felt they should. Not as the powerful clan wanted. Gloria, as upset as she was, seemed beyond comprehending that. "I know you mean well, Mrs. Westfield, but I really can't discuss this with you—"

Looking all the more fragile, Gloria continued as if Anne hadn't spoken. "It doesn't matter to me that Tim's adopted. I've cared for him since he was an infant." Her voice began to break. "I couldn't love him more if I'd carried him myself.

"I know you think you have a job to do. Tim has hired you and I respect that." Gloria's voice rose emotionally, "but there's a lot you don't know. And should." She shook her head miserably and dabbed at her eyes. "Tim hasn't been happy since his father died. He misses Frank desperately. He hasn't been getting along with his sisters or me, either, for that matter. I would hate to have anything add to that pain."

"So would I," Anne said softly.

"Perhaps if Frank hadn't died," Gloria whispered, "and if Tim were more involved in his own plans for the future, I would feel differently about his searching for his natural parents, but the way things stand..." Her eyes met Anne's in all earnestness. "He's focusing all his energies on this wild-goose chase, so much so that I'm afraid he's going to ruin his life."

What exactly did they think she was? Anne wondered, incensed. "I don't see how—"

"He was supposed to go to Harvard in the fall, but now he's decided against it. He says he might want to delay college for a year in order to search out his roots."

For a moment, Anne was at a loss. "I'm sorry," Anne said finally, able to understand Gloria's anguish, even if she had nothing to do with Tim's decision about his schooling. "I had no idea."

"That's why I'm talking to you now. So you will be aware of what's going on." Looking more high-strung than ever, Gloria lifted her head and looked straight at Anne. "I know I'm a total stranger to you but I'm asking—no, I'm begging—you for your help. Please, Anne. I want you to tell Tim what he wants can't be done."

Anne's heart was beating double-time. She wanted to assure herself she was doing what was right for Tim but now that she'd talked to Gloria she wasn't one hundred percent certain she was. Certainly Tim had a right to know about his natural parents, but maybe now wasn't the time. On the other hand, Tim wasn't likely to be dissuaded by anyone.

John was standing with a group of benefactors on the other side of the hall, but Anne had no doubt from the distracted expression on his face he knew exactly what was going on. He had set her up for this emotional confrontation with his sister-in-law. In fact, it was probably the whole reason he'd asked her here in the first place. Not because he'd wanted to get to know her, but because he'd wanted her to get to know them. She turned back to Gloria. "Tim is very determined. If I don't help him, he'll continue the search on his own or enlist someone else."

Without warning, the tears Gloria had been holding back slid down her face. John was at their side almost instantly, looking ten times more concerned than the situation warranted. "Everything okay?" He looked pointedly at his sister-in-law.

Anne wondered what he thought might have been revealed.

Gloria nodded and forced a smile as she dashed at the moisture with the back of her hand. "I'm fine, John," she said in a voice that shook. "Don't let me spoil your evening." Embarrassed, she moved away.

"I'm sorry about that," John murmured. "When Gloria said she wanted to talk to you, she assured me she could handle it. Obviously, she—" He broke off as he saw the distress on Anne's face. "I understand you have to do what you think is right," he finished pragmatically, obviously trying his best to be fair. "I don't want to pressure you."

"But you do wish I'd change my mind." Anne sighed, wishing she, too, could have had him on her side.

John spread his hands in an unapologetic gesture.

Before he could say another word, they were joined by a young woman in her early twenties, whom John promptly introduced as his executive assistant, Lily Carrington. Anne had only to look at Lily's face to know she idolized John.

"How's the mail-out on the new brochures coming?"

Lily shook her head, visibly discouraged. "Realistically we need another couple of days." Lily looked at Anne, explaining, "We're very shorthanded at the moment. We haven't gotten caught up since we won the primary. And what we're going to do about planning the Independence Day bash, I don't know. I went over the lists of things to be done this afternoon, and there's just no way I can handle it and execute my duties as office manager, too."

"We've been looking for someone to take over the organization of the July Fourth bash, to help take some of the burden off Lily," John said.

"But so far I haven't found anyone with the necessary social, business and managerial skills who's willing to sign on for just six weeks," Lily said with a sigh. She paused, looking at Anne. "You're a member of the local Better Business Bureau. You wouldn't happen to know of anyone, would you?"

"That depends. What exactly is involved?"

"A lot of organizing, mainly," Lily said.

"We need someone who can handle entertainment, guest lists, fireworks, publicity, security, the whole shebang," John said.

"And we need them soon," Lily stressed.

"Hmm." Anne could see why they were having trouble. Anyone who could do all that was very likely already working full-time. "Offhand, I can't think of anyone, but I'll give it some thought, ask around—"

"Thanks," Lily said, looking grateful. "With the Fourth just around the corner, we need all the help we can get."

Behind John, waiters were pushing through the doors, with trays of soup. "Looks like they're about to start," John said, his hand slipping beneath Anne's elbow once again. "We better get seated."

Dinner was surprisingly delicious, outshone only by John's fund-raising speech. "You're supposed to be campaigning for yourself tonight, John, not lobbying for more low-income housing," the owner of the local manufacturing company said when John had finished and people were once again milling around, waiting for the dance band to play.

"Can I count on your donation?"

The factory owner grinned. "All right. You've got one, from Unified Electronics."

"That was really impressive," Anne said as she and John walked off. "I wish I had your fund-raising skills."

His shoulder nudged hers as they approached the bar where white-coated waiters stood ready to fill their orders. "If you have a good cause, there's very little skill involved."

"Still, maybe you could give me a few pointers."

Without warning, he looked torn, as if he wanted to help her but couldn't because of her association with Tim.

"Sure," he said, after a moment, evading her direct glance. "When things calm down a bit in my personal life, I'd be glad to give you a few pointers. Do you want something?" He inclined his head toward the waiters.

"7UP, please."

"Make that two."

He handed her the first glass, his knuckles brushing hers lightly, then reached for the second. They moved slightly away from the bar, until they were well out of the path of others, and sipped their drinks. Across the room, the band finished tuning and began a soft sexy rendition of "Ain't Misbehavin'."

Anne was itching to dance. She loved slow music. But the image of herself in John's arms was more than a bit overwhelming. She decided to pick up the threads of their previous conversation. "What did you mean, 'when things settle down'?" she prodded curiously, enjoying their verbal sparring almost as much as she enjoyed standing next to him in the crowded banquet hall. "Is that after the election or when Tim and Gloria's problems are resolved?"

John's green eyes darkened. "After Tim's situation is resolved. He and Gloria have to be my first priority. I owe that to my brother."

His devotion, his closeness to family was completely at odds with his continuing refusal to help Tim. "You don't think much of my business, do you?"

"I didn't say that," he protested evasively, putting his empty glass aside. He placed his hand in hers.

"But you think I could make better use of my time?" She wanted to know what he thought and felt, and she wanted to distract herself from the intimate feel of his hand.

John frowned, his palm warming hers. "I can understand your satisfaction when your cases have happy endings," he said slowly.

"They do the vast majority of the time," Anne emphasized.

"You can't deny sometimes people are hurt by what you do." As Tim and Gloria and countless others would be if Anne persisted. When he saw she was finished with her drink he took her glass and set it aside.

Feeling flustered by his directness, she wet her lips, then wished she hadn't; his eyes had focused on her small, involuntary show of nervousness. "No, I can't."

He lifted a brow, studying her fiercely, as if the outcome of a great many things depended on her answer to his next question. "And you can live with the other less pleasant outcomes?" He tightened his hand on hers.

"Yes. It's not easy, but I do it." Anne paused as he slowly released his grasp on her hand. "I know it's a risk but I do it because I know I'm helping people resolve conflicts that are preventing them from getting on with their lives." Her own need to see her father prevented her from thinking of her future.

She saw respect in his eyes, but knew from the troubled set of his mouth he was still at war with his protective feelings about his family. "You still want me to drop Tim's case, don't you?" she asked, disappointed.

"In Tim's case his search for his natural parents is only exacerbating an already bad situation. He needs to deal with his adoptive father's death, figure out what he's going to do with his life, start getting excited about and planning his course of study in college. He has a mother who loves him. He already lost one father. I shudder to think what will happen should he lose another."

"I can't just drop the case, John."

"At least think about what I've told you," he urged.

Without warning, his assistant Lily Carrington appeared. "John, sorry to interrupt, but there's an exec from IBM who'd like to talk to you. He thinks maybe he can get his company to make a donation."

John excused himself, and seconds later Anne was standing alone. She wandered over to the punch bowl.

"Deserted, hmm?" a thirtyish-looking woman said. "Get used to it." At Anne's stunned glance, the woman stuck out her hand. "Hi. I'm Melinda Parker, John's ex-wife and a reporter for the Concord newspaper."

"Hi," Anne said, taking in the statuesque beauty with the glamorous fall of red hair, the wide blue eyes and the ivory skin. They shook hands briefly. Awed by Melinda's beauty, Anne continued to appraise the other woman openly. She wondered if John still had feelings for her, divorce or no.... "Anne Haynes."

"Have you been seeing John long?" Melinda asked. At Anne's shocked look, she reassured with a soft laugh, "Relax. I'm not going to challenge you to a cat fight. What John and I had was over a long time ago. My interest in you is strictly professional. They're going to run a picture of the two of you sitting together on the dais in the morning edition. I want to be correct, when I write this up in my column. So—" Melinda whipped out a notepad and pen and stood, poised to write.

"First of all," Anne corrected, "it isn't a date. We just met. And he asked me to attend."

"Okay." Melinda scribbled a note, then looked up. "What do you do?"

Anne paused, reluctant to be specific. Melinda might guess the rest and print something about Tim's search for his natural father. With a shrug, Anne evaded, "I'm a self-employed...researcher." It was as specific as Anne dared get.

"What's the name of your business?" When Anne didn't answer immediately, Melinda offered generously, "I'll give your business a free plug. It's not that I take this society column stuff seriously myself, you know. Just between you and me, I couldn't care less who wore what at what political fund-raiser, but they won't let me do anything else. Until I can get a job with the Associated Press—and that's not likely to happen until I can land a big enough story for the wire service—I'm stuck writing stories only socialites take seriously."

"I'm sorry. That must be frustrating," Anne murmured.

"It is. But it also can't be helped. So what do you say about the free advertising?"

Not about to elevate herself at Tim's expense, Anne said, "Thanks, but I'd rather not have my business mentioned on the society page."

"Why the hell not?" Melinda asked, her brow furrowing.

Anne shrugged and smiled, wary of being used to hurt John or his family. Melinda might appear glib at the moment, but there was no telling how scarred her divorce from John had left her. "I'm afraid it'll make me look frivolous," Anne said lightly. She dipped them each a glass of punch. "Besides, enough about me. I'd much rather know about you and John."

It was Melinda's turn to be put on the defensive, but she hid whatever unease she might be feeling. "There's not much to tell," Melinda told Anne. "We were married, it didn't work out, and now we're divorced."

But Melinda and John kept running into each other. "It must be hard, having to cover events in honor of your ex," Anne remarked sympathetically.

"It's not so bad," Melinda said with a candid smile, "if you don't mind being bored to death. Besides, I'm a professional. I'm supposed to be immune to personal problems when working."

"Easier said than done sometimes," Anne murmured.

"True, but I've managed to keep our personal differences out of my stories. I pride myself on my ability to treat John—in print—no differently than any other candidate."

That was impressive, Anne thought. She didn't know if she would be able to do the same. She had the feeling she'd be hurting too much after a divorce to be impartial. "He must appreciate that," she remarked. She remembered that Tim had told her things were a bit sticky between his ex-aunt and uncle.

Melinda pocketed her notebook and took a sip of her punch. "I guess. At first things were a little rocky." She paused reflectively, then gave Anne a sharp look. "Is that why you're so edgy, you think I'm out to get John through you or something?"

Anne shrugged. "The possibility had crossed my mind."

"Well, forget it. John wanted me to spend all my time campaigning for him—he was running for state representative then—and I wanted to get back to my career. I'd put it on hold, to work for his goals. I figured that was enough of a sacrifice."

Anne couldn't imagine sacrificing her own career goals for the sake of a husband, no matter how much she loved him. "And John didn't understand that?" Anne asked, surprised. He had seemed like such a compassionate person, in all other respects.

"Let's just say he wanted to be able to count on me when he needed me, the demands of my job aside.

So...we called it quits. In retrospect, it's the smartest thing we ever did together. I'm a lot happier now, and I think he is, too."

A shadow fell over them. "Ladies," John said, by way of greeting. Briefly he looked as though the two of them standing together, chatting up a storm, was his worst nightmare. Considering all Melinda had told her, Anne wasn't surprised.

"Hi, John." Melinda smiled up at him, visibly enjoying his discomfort. "Nice party."

He gave her a searching look. "You've met Anne, I see."

"Yes, we were having a nice chat." Melinda grinned at the increasingly distressed look on John's face and could put him on no longer. "Relax." She laughed. "I didn't say anything bad about you. *Ciao,* guys." With a careless wave, she moved off.

"I think I owe you a dance," John said, leading her to the dance floor. He swept her into his arms with the same masculine ease he did everything else, holding her just the right distance from him, not so loosely that it was awkward, not so closely that they nudged thighs and torsos.

"So what did she tell you?"

Anne studied the anxious look on his face and wondered if his ex-wife, for all her gregarious chatter, was to be trusted. Deciding he needed to lighten up a shade, she teased, "You say that as though you care what I think about you." And for a moment, oddly enough, she thought he did.

He bent low, so she could hear him, his warm breath brushing her ear, sending a shiver of renewed awareness down her spine. "It's no secret Melinda and I didn't part the best of friends."

He straightened and her eyes probed his. He took a deep breath, as if unsettled by the assessment he was sure she was making.

"She mentioned that, too," Anne bantered back quietly.

"So what else did she tell you?"

"Worried?" Anne teased.

The corners of his mouth twisted ruefully. "Let's just say I'm not used to my ex-wife giving an in-depth review of my character to my date."

Anne decided to put him out of his misery. Gently she reported, "Melinda said, essentially, you're a nice guy but that she just wasn't cut out to be a political wife, long-term." She watched as John relaxed visibly. "How long were the two of you together?"

"Five years."

She studied the sadness in his face. One song had ended, another had begun and they'd forgotten to stop and start dancing along with everyone else. "That's a long time," she commented sympathetically, wondering simultaneously what it would be like to be married.

"Yes, it was." John nodded, his grip on her tightening ever so slightly.

"Were you happy?" Anne was stunned to realize it made her the tiniest bit jealous to think they might have been.

"In the beginning, yes, I guess we were, but back then it was all new to her. She liked the glitz and glamour of it. The parties, the constant travel and entertaining. It was only later she began to miss her career and resent her lack of identity as anything except my wife."

That much made sense. Melinda was a very glamorous, sophisticated woman, exactly the type of person she would've expected John to pair up with. "Why didn't she just go back to work?"

"It wasn't that simple," John said. His hand brushed the bare skin of her back when another couple bumped into them. He replaced his hand at her waist. "Melinda wanted to be a political reporter. She couldn't do that objectively, in this state, as my wife. Neither of us wanted a commuter marriage. Maybe if she'd already been established as a political reporter when we met, it would've been different, but she wasn't." He shrugged, doing his best to conceal the hurt and loneliness he'd felt since and not quite managing.

"In the end, her career meant more to her than our marriage. By that time, I wanted out, too," he was quick to add. "I was tired of being blamed for holding her back professionally. Tired of her standing me up for even the most important occasion, so she could chase down a lead. So we parted." He sighed with what seemed to be relief. "And now she's working again, albeit not in the serious vein she'd like. Yet, anyway."

"And you're in the race for governor." A race Anne thought he was going to win.

"Yes."

The song ended and the two of them segued apart. Anne was surprised at how bereft she felt in the short span of time it took for another song to start and for him to hold her in his arms again. She fell into step, letting him lead. She soaked up the romantic strains of an old Cole Porter song she recognized as "You'd Be So Nice To Come Home To."

Holding back a sigh of contentment—how long had it been since she'd spent the night dancing in anyone's arms?—Anne struggled to tell him what she felt she must. "Melinda said they were going to run a picture of the two of us in the paper tomorrow."

"Did she tell you how the caption was going to read?"

"No, she did ask what I did for a living, though."

John froze, stopping so suddenly her thighs nudged the rock-solid line of his. Just what exactly was he so afraid she'd find out? "I told her I was self-employed but I didn't say doing what exactly."

"Why not?" He resumed dancing again. "It would've been a perfect opportunity for you to solicit donations and publicity."

Anne was achingly aware of that, but confidentiality was essential to her business ethics. "It also might have led to speculation about Tim. I didn't want that."

Respect glimmered in his eyes. When he spoke again, his voice was gruffly emotional, "Thanks."

"You're welcome." Anne met his eyes and wondered if he would ever be able to tell her all that was on his mind.

The dance ended. John was once again pulled away, this time by Gloria. To Anne's relief, Melinda had disappeared. Anne didn't see John again until it was time to leave. And even then they had no chance to talk privately until all the guests had disbanded and the two of them were walking to his car. The May night was crisp and clear, with a blanket of stars.

Anne now had a sense of what Melinda must have put up with during the years she was married to John. It hadn't been fun being ignored for large portions of the evening. When she went out, she was used to being the focal point of her date's attention.

"So," he said, tucking his hand beneath her elbow as they started across the hotel parking lot to his car, "you were there tonight. What are my chances of getting elected?"

Anne was all too aware of the light but possessive grasp he held on her arm. "I'm no pollster."

"Ah, but you are a smart, intuitive woman."

Her ego still stung from the easy way he'd been able to leave her during the evening. "You'll get a lot of votes," she said, careful to keep her voice neutral. After all, he was handsome, smart, politically correct, and he cared about people almost too much for his own good. Things might change if she exposed family secrets regarding Tim, though. Would it ruin his campaign? And how would he feel about her if it did?

John unlocked the car door, but didn't open it. "That's not what I want to know, Anne," he said softly. He tilted her chin up so she had no choice but to forget her treacherous thoughts and look into his light green eyes. "Will I get yours?"

At the unexpected intimacy in his tone and the deepening curiosity in his eyes, her heart skipped a beat. She had the sudden, strong impression he wanted to kiss her, then and there, and the equally strong impression that a very small, very daring part of her wanted him to.

But it would be a mistake to let him think there might ever be anything of substance between them. They had too many differences. He also had a full schedule and a rather skeptical view of her life's work. She stepped back away from him. "Technically, I'm not registered with either political party." She fastened her gaze on the silk of his black bow tie. "I vote for the best candidate." *Not the most handsome.*

His smile broadened and his voice dropped another intimate notch. "You're hedging—"

So she was. But what else could she say? So much depended on what she uncovered about Tim and John's role in the effort to keep his nephew in the dark about his Korean-American heritage. "I'll decide in November."

He studied her intently, the corners of his mouth turning up slowly. "But you will vote?" he pressed softly. This seemed very important to him.

Anne nodded, certain about that much. "Oh, yes." Having met John, she didn't know how she could resist.

Chapter Five

Around 2:00 a.m., John finally gave up and headed for the den. He wasn't going to be able to sleep, so he switched on all the lights, found the videotape of *Platoon* and slid it into the VCR. Settling down in his easy chair with a handful of chocolate chip cookies and a glass of milk, he started the movie. But even Charlie Sheen couldn't keep his mind off his problems, and moments later, he was as lost in thought as ever.

He had to face facts. Anne was not going to stop helping Tim. Smart as she was, she just might find out that Tim had been reared by his natural father all along. She might find out that John himself had been every bit as enmeshed in creating and maintaining the expanding web of lies as his brother had been. And she might resent him terribly, as would Tim, Gloria and his entire extended family.

John groaned. Frank hadn't meant to cause so much heartache but he had. And as always, John couldn't help but be angry at Frank about that. Damn it, why hadn't Frank kept his trousers zipped while he was stationed in Korea? Instead, fool that his older brother was, he had taken comfort from a native girl of nineteen. He had gotten her pregnant and ruined her life.

Of course, the calamity hadn't stopped there. Remorseful as always, Frank had decided to adopt his son, without telling anyone who Tim really was. Not that John could blame him for that. If Frank had told Gloria he'd managed to have a son during the year and a half he was away from her, after all the time Gloria had tried to get pregnant and been unable to, Gloria would have left him. Frank's political career would have been over before it began.

Frank had kept it a secret and enlisted John's help. And because he had loved his older brother, and knew how he would've felt if it had been *his* child, he had done what Frank had asked. He had kept Frank's secret without wondering whether he was right or wrong.

Until now. Until he'd had to look into Anne Hayne's exotically beautiful midnight-blue eyes and realize how much she'd resent and mistrust him if she ever found out the truth.

Even if he explained, she'd still tell him he'd had no right to help Frank perpetuate all those lies and that he should've known it would all come back to haunt them someday. She'd be right.

John sighed, his thoughts focusing on Anne. Damn, but she was beautiful. She didn't seem to know it, how much she affected him just by looking at him. He felt vaguely ashamed; he'd had an ulterior motive in asking her to the banquet. But he'd needed a chance to sway her over to his side, and the banquet had been it. Instead, he'd found himself captivated by her grace, gentleness, and inner strength. For the first time in his life, he'd met a woman with convictions that were every bit as strong and unshakable as his own. He'd met someone who cared about people as deeply as he did and who gave generously of herself to others, with no apparent thought to monetary or personal gain.

He'd been proud to have her seated next to him on the dais at the banquet, prouder still to introduce her as his date. In the white dress she'd worn, she'd looked spectacular. The beaded fabric had made the most of her golden skin tone and had shown off her slim, supple figure to perfection. His admiration hadn't stopped there. He'd been attracted to everything about her, from the incredible softness of her hands to the way she'd smelled of Shalimar, to the way she'd put up her luxuriant and silky black hair.

Holding her in his arms had been the sweetest pleasure. Not normally one to display affection in public, he'd found himself using every excuse to touch her, hold her hand, and keep her at his side. And he'd wanted to kiss her in the parking lot, next to his car. He knew she wasn't ready to be kissed. She sensed his dishonesty—didn't trust him—and rightfully so.... He'd reined in the impulse and stifled his desire. But thinking about the way she looked in that dress, made him ache again. He wanted to be with her night and day until the time was right and he could kiss her.

If only there was some way to make Anne do what he wanted concerning Tim, without telling her the truth. But there wasn't. She would feel Tim had a right to know.

Suppose Tim did find out, John thought worriedly, getting up to pace the room restlessly. What then? How would Tim cope with that news, knowing that everything his father had ever told him about his early life had been a lie? How would Gloria cope? Would her feelings about Tim change if she knew he was Frank's natural son and the product of her husband's infidelity? John sighed. If Anne continued her search, it would rip his family apart. Somehow, he had to stop her.

By morning, he knew what he had to do. Devotion to family had motivated him to keep Frank's secret. Family might be what he needed to make Anne stop. Fortunately Carl and Celia Haynes were easy to find. He stopped by their house, unannounced, the next morning. To his relief, the woman who opened the door looked every bit as kindhearted and decent as he could have hoped. Taking in her chestnut curls, which were streaked liberally with silver, and her soft gray eyes, he felt his hopes for an immediate solution rise. "Mrs. Haynes?" Holding out his hand, he introduced himself politely. "I'm John Westfield."

Celia clasped a hand to the front of her cotton sweater. "I know who you are!" she gasped, looking utterly surprised. "I've seen you on television. You're running for governor."

John grinned. His presence often caused reactions like this, but he never quite got used to it. "Yes." He looked past her to the inviting interior of their small but well-kept home. "May I come in? I'd like to speak to you about your daughter Anne."

"I'm sorry. Where are my manners! Certainly you can come in." She motioned for him to have a seat on the sofa. "Just let me get my husband. Carl!" she called, rushing off in the direction of the kitchen, where something delicious seemed to be baking. "John Westfield is here!"

Seconds later, a man in a flannel shirt and jeans appeared. Not wasting time with unnecessary introductions, he greeted John warmly. "You've already got our vote, you know."

"Thanks." John smiled. It was hard-working, decent people like the Hayneses John most wanted to help.

"He's here to talk to us about Anne," Celia explained. She entered the room, carrying a tray that held coffee and freshly baked cookies. As she doled out the aromatic treats, Carl gave John an anxious look. "She's not in any trouble, is she?"

"Well—" John hesitated as he sipped the freshly brewed coffee. Suddenly it wasn't so easy to talk to Anne's parents; he didn't want to hurt them. "Actually it's about her business." Briefly he filled the older couple in on his worry about his nephew. He finished, "In my opinion, Tim is not dealing with his grief about the loss of his father, and he's using this quest to avoid dealing with it."

"Have you told Anne how you felt?" Celia asked cautiously, still siding with her daughter.

"Yes. It hasn't helped."

Carl regarded John thoughtfully. "Is that why you took Anne to that dinner last night?"

The man was nothing if not direct. "Yes," John answered honestly, seeing no reason to hide his devotion to his own family from the Hayneses. "I thought perhaps if Anne met Tim's mother and saw how much Gloria loved Tim, it would change her mind."

"But it didn't," Celia guessed.

"No," John admitted with regret. He didn't want to continue to be at odds with Anne. Nor did he want to be at odds with Anne's family.

Celia leaned forward to freshen his coffee. "I don't know what to tell you, John, except that Anne's a very sensitive and caring woman, who's very committed to helping her clients."

"She wouldn't do anything to hurt that nephew of yours," Carl added, throwing his full support to his daughter.

John knew that, too. But just because Anne didn't mean to hurt Tim, didn't mean she wouldn't.

"Anne's commitment to other Amerasians comes from the fact that she knows firsthand what it's like to be orphaned with little or no memory of her biological parents," Celia explained. "Whether we like it or not, the possibility of tracing one's roots and finding a natural family is not a project most adopted children can turn their backs on," Celia said.

John guessed not. "What about her own situation? Has Anne ever researched that?"

Without warning, Carl and Celia exchanged a tension-laced look. Celia explained how Anne had lost her mother when she was five. "The last she heard, her father was still alive. She's been trying to track him down for nearly a decade."

"In fact, it was her frustration with the process that initially prompted her to open her own agency," Carl added protectively.

John wondered what it would be like to not know who his real father was. He couldn't imagine it. He could see how not knowing would nag a person. But he could also see that Anne had been adopted by two people who genuinely loved her. Shouldn't that be enough? Apparently not for Anne. And maybe not for most people. Including himself? "But she hasn't found him?"

"Not yet," Carl confirmed, a worried set to his mouth.

"Or if she has," Celia admitted quietly, "she hasn't told us. Yet, anyway."

They sat in silence. John struggled to understand how Anne's search for her natural father had affected her relationship with Carl and Celia. He could see they loved her dearly, but he could also see their relationship with her was currently strained. They were unable to talk openly as they would've liked with her. His curiosity about Anne and her traumatic past grew. "If you don't mind my asking, how old was Anne when she was adopted?"

This, Carl found much easier to talk about. "She was five. And let me tell you, she was a very bright child. Nevertheless, she had a hard time adjusting to this country. She had to deal with the trauma of adjusting to a new culture and learn the language. She never complained, but it was very hard for her."

"Of course we did everything we could to help her," Celia continued. "Fortunately our own two children were already in college by then, so we had plenty of time to devote to Anne."

She shook her head regretfully and confessed in a troubled voice, "Even so, we were never as close to her as we were to the older two. It was as if Anne had built a wall around her heart, so she wouldn't get hurt again. She was that way with all of us, her brother and sister, too."

Whether she'd meant to or not, John realized, Anne had made her adoptive parents feel ineffective and second-best. Maybe if he'd been in the same situation he would have reacted similarly. He knew his loyalty to his own family went very deep. If he'd been abandoned by his father and then orphaned by his mother, would he have been able to accept a new family, never mind one from a completely different country and culture? Or would he have retained a deep, unshakable allegiance to the past, the way Anne apparently had?

"I wish we could be of more help to you," Celia said.

"But Anne needs to do what she feels is right," Carl continued.

Realizing he had taken up more than enough of their time, John rose. "Thanks for talking to me."

Celia walked him to the door. "I hope things work out for your family," she said softly, shyly, in a way that reminded him very much of Anne at her sensitive best.

"Thanks. So do I."

ANNE SIFTED THROUGH the paperwork her friend at the Catholic orphanage in Seoul had sent her, unable to believe what she was reading. Tim's mother, far from being the young prostitute John had supposed, had come from a very wealthy family. The protected only daughter of a South Korean businessman, Son-ja Kim had fallen into an illicit love affair with a young officer and had become pregnant within a few months. The family had pressed for marriage, but the officer, already married himself and the son of very influential parents, had refused.

Betrayed by her lover, at the mercy of her angry, embarrassed family, Tim's young mother had been spirited off to a convent to have her baby in utter secrecy. Despite the shame of being an unwed mother in a highly moral society, Son-ja Kim had wanted to keep her child, but the Kim family had intervened and taken away her child directly after birth.

Shortly thereafter, a suitable marriage had been arranged by her family, a large dowry paid, and she was forced to marry a much older man, Sundar Hasegawa. Almost two decades later, she was still married to him and living in Japan. She was also, reportedly, the mother of two very pampered school-age children.

Anne was shocked but happy. Tim's mother had never wanted to give him up! Surely, Anne thought, Son-ja Kim Hasegawa would want to see her son now! All Anne had to do was contact her, let her know her son was alive and well and looking for her, too.

Determined to reunite these two people who never should have been torn apart so heartlessly, Anne started typing with a vengeance. The Westfields might not agree, but she knew she was doing the right thing. She was just finishing her letter to Tim's mother when the phone rang. It was Lily Carrington. "Hi, Anne, is John there?"

Anne looked guiltily at the letter in her hand. "No," she said, annoyed at herself for feeling panicked about doing her job. She paused, aware her heart was beating very rapidly. "Is he on his way over?"

"Well, I thought so," Lily said, "but it's so crazy over here—we've got a ton of volunteers stuffing envelopes—I can't hear myself think. Let me go take another look at the itinerary he left on his desk." She put down the phone. Anne could hear the confusion in the background, the sounds of voices, clicking keyboards, noisy printers and ringing phones.

"Oh, darn, I'm sorry," Lily apologized. "I was looking at this morning's schedule, not this afternoon's! I'm sorry to have bothered you—"

"Are you sure you're looking at the right schedule? John wasn't over here this morning."

"He wasn't?" Lily repeated, puzzled. "It says right here. Haynes. 3314 South Maple Street. Oh, no." She gave a small short gasp. "That's not your address."

"No, it's my parents'," Anne remarked, equally confused. "Why was John at my parents' home?" Surely John wouldn't have involved them in his campaign to get her to stop helping Tim. She would feel very betrayed and more than a little angry, if that were the case. She hoped it wasn't.

There was a telling silence on the other end of the phone. "I don't know, Anne. Maybe—maybe he was talking to them about a donation for the low-income housing."

"My parents?" Anne repeated in disbelief. She knew with a certainty that went gut-deep that Lily was effecting a cover-up on her beloved boss's behalf.

The din in the background increased. Lily had to shout to be heard over the hum of voices, "Listen, Anne, I've got to go! The volunteers are only going to be here another hour and we've got five hundred envelopes left! Sorry for bothering you!" The phone clicked as she severed the connection.

Her heart thudding heavily, Anne replaced the receiver. Damn John Westfield, for involving her parents in what should have been a private business matter. How could he have done that to her? One thing was certain: he wouldn't do it again. She'd see to that.

The lights in his office building were on when she drove up, but only two cars remained in the lot.

"Anne," Lily said when she saw Anne storm in, "is something the matter?"

Ignoring the concern on Lily's face, Anne looked straight at John, her temper flaring out of control. "You bet something's the matter! John Westfield, we have to talk!"

Chapter Six

"How dare you involve my family!" Anne said the moment after Lily had grabbed her things and left the office.

The muted sound of a car door closing, a car starting and moving off, filled the silence. John stared at her flushed face reluctantly, his eyes locked with hers in silent unrelenting battle. Not about to back down, he rested both hands on his waist and released a long-suffering breath. He knew he shouldn't have gone there. Involving her family had been unconscionable. But dammit, she'd left him no choice! "I'm trying to protect my nephew," he said stiffly.

Anne knew all about that kind of protection; it suffocated people, and made their pain, their internal misery, and their sense of loss and loneliness all the worse. Had Carl and Celia helped instead of thwarted her, she might have been able to find Robert Ryan years ago. But they hadn't, and at twenty-eight she was still struggling to figure out who she was and where she'd come from.

Home Free

Advancing on John boldly, she shook her hair away from her face and echoed with cutting disdain, "Protect him? That's a laugh. What you're trying to do is keep Tim in the dark." Not that he would succeed by involving her folks. All he had accomplished with that was to anger and alienate her.

He regarded her sharply, wishing like hell he wasn't so aware of the disarray of her glossy black hair or the mingled hurt and fury in her dark blue eyes. Blowing out a weary breath, he said, "Look, I've tried to explain to you that this quest of Tim's is only going to hurt him."

"You don't know that." In fact, she was willing to bet that Tim and his mother would have a happy reunion.

John's thoughts went to the duplicity he had helped his older brother perpetrate. "The hell I don't!" John answered, jerking loose the knot on his tie.

His inner torment suddenly made everything so much clearer. Her intuition spoke to her, loud and clear. "You've already looked into this," she accused. "Haven't you?"

"Don't be ridiculous!" John said gruffly. "I'm just telling you his mother might very well turn out to be someone Tim doesn't want to meet!"

Undaunted, Anne circled close. She could smell the spicy, masculine scent of his cologne and see the faint shadow of evening beard on his face. "There's only a chance of that."

His head lifted and his light green eyes bore into hers. "Even a slight chance of things backfiring is too much to take at this point."

Anne slid a hip onto the far corner of his desk and leaned toward him casually. "Suppose I could promise you otherwise?" she said softly, thinking of what she had discovered thus far about Son-ja Kim Hasegawa. "Would you stop interfering?"

John's face went white when he realized she was no longer fishing for information. "I've found her," Anne said.

"And his father?"

"Not yet, but I'm working on that, too."

John shook his head grimly, looking as though he had descended into a nightmare from which there was no awakening. Aware of his tenseness, Anne's heart began a slow, heavy beat. She knew he thought her a meddling witch. She knew he wanted to pitch her bodily out the nearest window, but it was too late for that. The damage had already been done, and it was time he knew that, too.

"And I've taken the first step in contacting her," she announced optimistically, ignoring the shock on his face and the way he grimaced. He would feel better once he knew what she did, that the situation was destined to have a happy ending. "She didn't want to give Tim up—"

You're wrong about that, John thought, remembering what his brother had told him shortly after his return to the States. *She feels like her life is ruined. The nuns told me Son-ja and her family don't want any part of her Amerasian child.* John faced Anne, furious it had gone this far, this fast. "How do you know this?" he demanded. "Who have you talked to?" What made her think she'd discovered the truth?

Anne was silent. To disclose her underground connections might be to jeopardize them and that she wouldn't do. She had worked too long and too hard to find people willing to help her.

"All right," John said harshly, when he realized she had no intention of answering him. "What'll it take to get you off this case? You said you needed money for Answers, Inc. How much?"

"You're insulting." Anne hopped down from the desk and headed past him, for the door.

John moved to block her path. When she tried to step around him, she found herself backed up against the door, her body trapped between the unyielding warmth of his and the hardness of the solid oak behind her.

"I mean it, Anne," he repeated, his outstretched arms on either side of her. "How much?"

He spoke as if this were the only solution. She heard the censure in his voice and hated it. "I don't want your money!" Unable to bear the betrayal she saw in his eyes, she turned her head to the side.

He was too close. If she moved even an inch, their bodies would be pressed together, hip to hip, thigh to thigh. She wished now she had never come.

He slipped a hand beneath her chin and tilted her face up, so she had no choice but to look into his eyes.

"If not money, then what do you want?" His voice was as soft and yet relentless as his grip.

"To do my job!" Anne said. She heard her voice tremble, but was unable to do anything about it. The day had been a rough one. John had betrayed her, she'd fought with her parents... and now this. There was no path she could take that would make everyone happy. No path she could take where no one would be hurt.

Seeing her determination to continue on the path she had chosen, John backed off slightly, all the while retaining his hold on her. His voice condemning her, he warned, "You can't help Tim this way."

She felt herself bristle. He was so autocratic. Why, she didn't know. Normally he was so compassionate, so in touch with people's needs and feelings. How could he be so blind to the desires of his nephew? Or *was* he? "How do you know I can't help him?" she persisted.

"Because I know, all right?" John snapped back, raking both his hands through his hair.

And maybe he did, Anne realized, working hard to slow the gallop of her pulse. She knew from her years of sleuthing that something was behind his panic. "What are you hiding?"

John turned away from her, moving to hide his expression from her scrutiny. No longer so ready to leave, Anne followed him. "What do you know about this that I don't?"

John swung around to face her, and his eyes met hers. She saw the honesty in his eyes and knew the first hurdle had been crossed.

"Enough to know Tim and my whole family will be very hurt if you continue with this. Please, Anne, I'm begging you." He spoke softly, urgently, in a way that, despite everything, made her want to comply. *"Don't do this. Don't open a Pandora's box."*

His calculated attempt to buy her off was easy to resist. Not this. "It's too late," Anne said, wishing she could help John and Tim simultaneously. She was more aware than ever of the tension crackling between them. She wished she had somewhere to run. "I already express-mailed a letter to Tim's mother in Tokyo, telling her everything." *And thank heaven I did because if I hadn't, I don't know if I could have found the strength to do so now, not with you looking at me this way, as though your heart is about to break.*

John's face paled. He released a soft, defeated breath. His hands clenched into fists at his side. "Tokyo? That's where she's living?"

Anne nodded. They regarded each other quietly. She knew she had disappointed him deeply, that he'd thought he had more time to work on her. She was surprised at how much it hurt her.

"It's late. I'd better go." She pivoted on her heel. She didn't dare let the worried look on his face get to her; he might actually change her mind about continuing the search for Tim's father.

"Anne, wait—" His low voice, so laced with reason, stopped her.

He had a lot of incentives for calling her back. Guilt—he felt lousy for what he'd done to her. Fear—she still didn't know about Frank. But it was more than that. She interested him in a way no woman ever had. Because there seemed so many layers to her and because she'd been through so much in her lifetime, he wanted to know everything about her. And, crazy as it seemed, he wanted her to understand him. His desire to know her was selfish, but there it was. Undeniable. Solid. And it wasn't going to go away.

"I'm sorry." His touch was as soft and compelling as he could make it when he caught up with her. He placed a gentle hand on her shoulder and turned her reluctant body to face him. He saw the curiosity in her eyes, the hesitation. "We can't let the evening end like this."

Anne sighed. She didn't want to end it badly, either, but she was also aware of the danger of calling a truce with him, even a temporary one. There was still much at stake, and she couldn't forget they were on opposite sides of the fence, and that she had a professional obligation to Tim that was contrary to everything John wanted.

"I should never have gone to your parents that way," John apologized sincerely. "You're right to be angry with me about that."

"Yes," Anne agreed succinctly.

They both fidgeted. Anne released a pent-up breath and rubbed at the tenseness in her slender neck. John gave her a wan smile. "Maybe it's time we called a truce."

Anne studied him, not as willing to shift gears as he, even if it was politic to do so. "Why?"

Wishing she'd smile at him, just a little, John grinned and said dryly, "Because we'll draw blood soon if we don't."

"Does that mean you'll lay off visiting my folks?"

It was clear to John the whole deal hinged on his acceptance of her terms. "Okay, I promise, no more visits to your folks. But you have to give me something, too."

Anne took a deep breath, telling herself she was in control of this situation. "What?"

Sensing her nervousness, he made his voice as gentle and persuasive as he could. "Time to get to know me. To let me know you. Like it or not we are in this together, Anne. On opposite sides of the fence to be sure, but if we don't work out some way to handle each other, without bringing the whole house down around us, it's Tim and Gloria who'll suffer the most. I don't want that. Do you?"

"No." She had to admit he made her lose sight of her normal professional attitude at times. She sensed she did the same to him.

He hesitated and an expression passed over his face she couldn't identify. "Want to get some dinner?"

"All right," she said after a moment, concerned her acceptance would be misconstrued on his part. "But it's Dutch treat." She was doing this only because she did not want him as her enemy.

He grinned and took her elbow. "You don't have to pay, you know," he remarked, looking into her eyes. "After all, I asked."

"That's okay." Anne shifted her grip on her handbag. "I prefer it this way." If he paid for dinner, it'd begin to feel like a date. It was going to be hard enough to keep her distance from him as it was. She was too attracted to him in an elemental way, as was evidenced by the shivers that ran down her skin at just the light touch of his hand beneath her elbow.

"The self-sufficient type, hmm?" His voice was a teasing rumble in her ear.

Anne nodded, more serious about that than John knew. Ever since her real mother had died, she hadn't felt secure unless she knew she would make it on her own.

"Would it insult your independence if I asked to drive us both? Then I'll bring you back here later to get your car."

Knowing she'd look unnecessarily wasteful in these energy-conscious times if she refused, she said, "Okay."

They decided on Peter Christian's Tavern in New London. Thirty minutes later, they were settled in a wooden booth in the cramped, convivial quarters. A gathering place for the young, the atmosphere was cozy and relaxed. After poring over the menus, they decided on bowls of thick, spicy tortilla soup and the restaurant's specialty, "Peter's Father's Favorite Sandwich," a concoction brimming with roast beef, cheese, onion, tomato, spinach and horseradish.

Noticing John was tugging on his tie, Anne remarked lightly, "You could probably lose the tie."

John took it off and dropped it into the pocket of his jacket. "It's hard to go anywhere without feeling self-conscious these days."

Anne understood that only too well. When they'd walked in, the hostess as well as several patrons and their waitress had all paid homage to John in one way or another. Thankfully, the attention had eased once they were seated. "I guess that's the price you pay for having such a high profile," Anne remarked lightly, trying not to notice the dark tufts of hair that sprang from the open V of his shirt.

"I take it politics isn't something you'd choose for yourself?" He stirred sugar into his iced tea.

Anne shook her head. "I wouldn't bear up under the constant scrutiny."

Briefly he looked disappointed, as if she'd somehow let him down by not sharing his enthusiasm for public life.

Reminding herself this was just an effort to cement the truce between them, not a date, Anne steered the conversation back to safer ground. "If you hadn't been reared a Westfield, would you have chosen politics?"

"I think, no matter what, I would have selected one of the helping professions. Been a cop or a doctor, maybe. Probably not a lawyer or a teacher. What about you? Was there anything else you wanted to do?"

"Not really." She had been consumed with curiosity about her past as long as she could remember. That and only that had driven her choice of careers.

He'd given her an opening, but she was more comfortable talking about him than herself. "What was your childhood like?"

"A veritable zoo, but the best times were spent out at the Westfield family compound." His thick, luxuriant lashes widened and he flashed her his million-dollar politician's grin. "You've probably seen pictures of it."

"Yes. It's quite luxurious." And very different from her own parents' home.

He smiled at her, and this time she smiled back, just a little. "What was your childhood like?"

Anne shrugged, wishing she could say it had been as easy and happy as his had apparently been. "Protected, pampered, lonely."

He frowned, looking both puzzled and sympathetic. "No friends?"

Anne dropped her gaze. She didn't want his scrutiny or his pity. "No, no friends, not right away. I was too different."

John weighed her nonchalance with the flicker of hurt he had seen in her eyes. He knew how cruel kids could be. He could imagine the kids making fun of her and how that must have hurt. Suddenly it was all he could do to stay on his side of the booth, to not reach out and drag her into his arms for a warm, comforting hug. "Surely Carl and Celia helped you to fit in?"

Anne forced a wan smile and tried to look jovial. "Of course they did. They bought me the latest clothes and had my hair cut and permed in a gypsy shag that was so popular at the time."

He couldn't imagine that. He liked the way her hair was now, so long and thick and black and silky soft. He liked the way the golden hue of her skin contrasted with the dark blue-black of her eyes and the wild exotic blend of her Shalimar perfume and skin.

"They helped me learn how to read, write and speak English properly; they taught me slang. They acclimated me to popular television programs like *The Brady Bunch* and *The Partridge Family*."

"Did it help?"

Anne smiled, accepting that the difficulty she had been through was natural and to be expected. Culture shock, they called it. "Eventually," she admitted. She still hadn't met a man who understood her deep inside, not the way John was trying to.

By the time their sandwiches arrived, Anne felt much calmer. She had known from the beginning they would never agree about her work, but that didn't mean they couldn't be friends. They would just have to be careful not to discuss topics they disagreed so strongly about.

John suddenly ducked his head. "Uh-oh, I've been recognized again."

And it looked, Anne thought, as if the people in question were not going to vote for him. "Is it hard going out alone now?" Anne asked.

John nodded, his eyes meeting hers. "I thought I was prepared for it, having been a state representative all these years, but I wasn't. Everywhere I go these days I'm recognized and eventually approached for an autograph, favor or complaint."

"I thought politicians reveled in that kind of attention."

"I guess I do." He traced an imaginary pattern on the table beside his plate. "But I'm like anyone else. Without time off from the job, I get very stressed."

"I get stressed out, too, when I'm overworked or under a lot of pressure," Anne admitted. "Sometimes I say or do things that I later regret."

"We all do," John said, letting her know with a smile it wasn't something she should agonize over, in his opinion.

"And?"

He shrugged. "I apologize, make amends and move on."

She envied his ability to let go of things so easily. She had never been able to do that.

Both had finished their meal, but John liked sitting in the darkened restaurant with Anne and was in no hurry to leave. He took another sip of his iced tea, wondering all the while what her life was really like. Was she happy? Or was she, like him, still searching for that elusive something that would make his life complete? "Do you work very long hours?"

"Very," Anne admitted, wishing he'd quit looking at her so intently. She was unable to remember when she had enjoyed a simple dinner so much or the company she was with. She dropped her gaze shyly, her hand curling nervously around the napkin in her lap. "The past two years I've been lucky. I've only had to work at Answers, Inc. The six years prior to that, I held down two jobs to make ends meet." She sighed, lifting her eyes to his. "Unfortunately I may have to go back to work as a linguist in the next month or so." She'd run up a lot of bills tracing Robert Ryan, more than she could pay....

"That makes you unhappy?" he asked in a soft, sympathetic voice.

Anne nodded. She hated dividing her time. "What I'd really like is something part-time or a donation for my foundation." Once he found out more about the nature of her work and her record of successes, Anne had hopes Robert Ryan would not only respect and appreciate what she did, but contribute a sizable amount to her.

John looked thoughtful as the waitress came over and poured them both some more tea. "What about the organizational job that's open in my campaign? We still need someone to put together the July Fourth bash. And as Lily says, the sooner the better."

Anne had no doubt she could do the job. Compared to starting her own agency, putting together a party would be a snap. She studied him cautiously. "Why would you want to do this for me?"

He grinned and reached across the table. "Maybe I want you under my thumb." As he spoke, he lightly tapped the back of her hand with his thumb.

Anne shook her head, knowing this was not true. Dominating, he was not. She smiled. "Try again." *And be straight with me this time.*

His thumb stilled. His eyes grew serious. "Maybe I want you near."

That she could believe. She was beginning to feel that way, too. She didn't want to admit that to him, though, because of the vulnerable position it would put her in. "Try again."

"Because Lily's going to have a nervous breakdown if I don't relieve her of some of the responsibility she's been carrying lately and because we're beginning to be friends."

Were they really? Anne wondered. If not, the potential of friendship was definitely there, their ongoing argument over Tim's situation aside.

"So is that a yes or a no?" John asked, moving his hand away from hers.

Anne straightened, pressing her spine against the unyielding back of the booth. "I still have some cases besides Tim's." Lei's friend Trong, for one.

"If you think you can manage both jobs simultaneously, I have no problem with that."

"And I also have a trip to Minneapolis scheduled this weekend—"

"What's in Minneapolis?" He looked worried and, Anne thought, perhaps a little jealous as well.

She was afraid to say anything about finding her father. After searching so long and hard, talking might jinx it. "I've got personal business there I've got to get cleared up."

"How long will you be gone?"

She sent him a grateful glance. "I don't know. A couple of days." Maybe longer, she thought hopefully, if my father wants me to stay....

"But you could be on the job by Monday morning?"

Anne nodded. No matter how well things went with Robert Ryan, sooner or later she would have to come back to the life she had carved out for herself here. "Monday would be fine. I could be there first thing."

"All right," John said smiling. He signaled the waitress for their check, "Monday it is."

"YOU HIRED HER without even talking to me?" Lily asked the next morning, visibly shaken and hurt.

John realized he had made a giant error. "I thought you wanted someone right away, to take some of the pressure off."

"I do, but, John—"

"What?" John prodded impatiently, when Lily didn't go on.

"Never mind. When does she start?"

"On Monday."

Lily frowned. "Why not this week?"

"She has to go to Minneapolis."

"On a case?"

"Personal business."

"Oh." Lily latched on to that, like a bloodhound on a trail. "Like a boyfriend there?" she asked, point-blank.

I hope not, John thought. He'd only known Anne a short while, but the thought of her with anyone else was definitely not one he liked. "She didn't say." Whatever it was, though, it had seemed important to her. Very important.

"MR. RYAN will see you now, Ms. Haynes."

"Thank you."

Anne stood on shaking knees and made her way to the carved oak door. Stepping into the luxurious office, she focused on Robert Ryan. Her first thought was that he had aged. Her second thought was that she would have known him anywhere. He had thick dark hair, streaked liberally with gray, cut in military style. He was tall and imposing, with patrician features and arresting blue eyes. And although he was pushing sixty, he hadn't let his figure go to seed. His abdomen and chest were military trim and fit.

"Ms. Haynes." He smiled at her and reached across the desk to shake her damp, trembling hand.

Anne nodded, feeling ridiculously close to tears and more tongue-tied than ever before. Dear God, she thought, I can't fall apart now.

"Why don't you have a seat?" His expression was kind. He gestured to a chair upholstered in a soft dove-gray-and-white jacquard. She sank into it gratefully, aware she was still shaking from head to toe.

"I understand you're here to see me about donating money to your agency, Answers, Inc. I'll be frank with you." He frowned as if searching for words that wouldn't offend her. "I've had some experience with such agencies. I've found they extract enormous sums of money from people and in the end do very little good."

"You're wrong," Anne interrupted, feeling both stung and resentful. "I've had a number of successes." And her reunion with Robert Ryan would be one more. "And that's why I'm here," Anne continued nervously. "Because I wanted to tell you—" Now that the moment was finally here, she didn't know exactly how to say it. In the end, she just blurted it out. "Mr. Ryan—Dad—I am the little girl you left behind in Saigon."

Before she'd even finished, he was on his feet. "You're lying," he said flatly. He was furious, his entire bearing rigid. "My little girl died—"

"No," Anne responded in confusion, tears of mixed joy and pain flowing down her face. "I'm not lying. I am that little—"

"And now I suppose you're going to tell me you remember me from then, too," Robert Ryan said in a hard, sarcastic voice. If he recognized any possible resemblance to himself or her mother, he didn't show it.

"No," Anne said. This was her worst nightmare. "But I remember my mother Anh Sengsouvoung, who died when I was five. I remember the shrine she kept of your photo in our apartment and how desperately she prayed you would come and rescue us. I remember she said you had *promised* to come back. And I remember how you never did."

Her father stared at her in shock, clearly wanting to believe her, but unable to. His lips thinned in reproach. "I don't know who you are or what you hope to gain by this hoax, young woman, but I want you to know I think it's very cruel. I loved my Saigon family. I *wanted* to get them out." His voice shook with rage. "It took years to cut through the paperwork and by the time I managed to get through the red tape both my lover and her child had died of malaria."

"That's what I'm trying to tell you. My mother died." Anne placed her hand over her heart. "I didn't."

"You're lying!"

"No!" Anne said, so hurt she was barely able to breathe.

"Get out of my office," Robert Ryan thundered, pounding his fist on his desk. "And don't ever come back again!"

Because she had no choice, Anne left. She tried several times after that to get in touch with him, but to no avail. In bitter defeat, she left for New Hampshire.

When her doorbell rang Sunday night, it was all she could do to make herself answer it.

"Bad trip?" John asked quietly, concerned.

Anne nodded, feeling near tears again and inexplicably as though she wanted to throw herself into his arms for a long, heartfelt hug. "The worst."

He cradled the stack of papers in his hands, looking as awkward and distressed as she felt. "I guess this isn't the time to be dropping off work," he said lamely.

"No. It's fine." Drowning in self-pity would not help anything, and besides she needed someone to get her mind off her troubles. "Come on in."

In a long-sleeved rugby shirt and jeans, he looked rugged and fit and more accessible than when he was dressed in his usual suit and tie. Reminding herself this was strictly a business visit, she asked, "What have you got for me?" She eyed the huge stack of manila folders with both interest and dread, remembering how much she hated work that took her away from her agency.

"Everything Lily has compiled so far. Bids from various caterers, guest lists, security firms and so forth. I thought you'd want to take a look at everything you're going to have to do but I can see this isn't a good time." He paused, knowing he wasn't fooling either of them. He had come because he couldn't wait to see her, and because he had been wondering all weekend about her trip to Minneapolis. "Is everything okay?" he asked finally. "Is there anything I can do?"

A very private person, Anne normally would have brushed off his attempts to help her, but as she looked into his light green eyes, she suddenly knew she had to talk to him. Before she could stop herself, the whole story came tumbling out.

John joined her on the sofa and listened quietly. When she was finished, he said, "Do you have any proof Robert Ryan is your father?"

"Just a letter from a retired nurse in Saigon who knew my mother years ago, but nothing concrete that he couldn't somehow refute.

"It's funny, I never pictured myself getting rejected that way," Anne continued. "It hurt worse than I ever imagined." Because it had, she was finally beginning to understand John's fear about his nephew. What if Tim's situation worked out in the same way? Would John be able to forgive her? Would Tim? Would she be able to forgive herself?

"I'm sorry." He covered her hands with his own, the warmth of his skin transmitting to hers.

"So am I," she said quietly, still wishing it had gone better. But looking back, she didn't know what else she could have done.

"Maybe he'll be more receptive when he has a chance to think about it," John offered hopefully at last.

"I don't think so," Anne confessed miserably. "He seemed pretty adamant." All those years...now all her hopes and dreams had been crushed.

"So what now?" he asked softly.

Anne shrugged. Tears stung her eyes. "I don't know. I go on I, guess."

"You know what you need?"

Anne sighed, some of her misery fading. "No, but I suppose you're going to tell me, anyway."

He grinned. "Damn straight I am." Taking her hand, he drew her upright and away from the sofa. "It's time you got away from all this."

She knew she was not going to be very good company, no matter what they did or where they went, and so she was reluctant to say yes.

"Go out with me, Anne." His eyes met and held hers. "Please."

A few hours, what could it hurt? she thought. On the other hand, John was now her employer. But that was just for six weeks, until the Fourth of July was over. After that she'd probably never see him. "Okay. Just give me time to freshen up a little."

He was standing at the bookcases, surveying the fiction titles that were crowded among the phone books from Asia when she returned. "Doesn't having your office in your home get to you?" he asked.

As usual, he'd hit the nail right on the head. Anne nodded. "Sometimes it's a pain. I feel like I can never get away from my work. Sometimes it's a luxury. I can work in my pajamas at midnight if I want."

"I'd like to see that," he said, wiggling his brow and giving his best Groucho Marx impression.

She pantomimed a teasing blow to the solid wall of his chest and went to get her jean jacket. "Where to?" She had a feeling this was going to be fun.

"You'll see."

To her delight, he retained his air of mystery until they pulled up in front of the brightly lit lot on the other side of town. "Animal Kingdom Putt-Putt!"

"Don't you like miniature golf?"

She glanced at the kiddie decor. "I don't know. I never tried it." She hoped he didn't expect her to be fabulous. The Westfield clan might all be sports nuts, but she'd spent much of her youth in either the library or the choir room. She wasn't particularly athletically inclined.

"Trust me," John promised, wrapping a reassuring hand around her shoulders. He guided her toward the ticket booth. "With my expert instruction you'll be a pro in no time."

"It's not necessary to put *both* arms around my waist," Anne remarked dryly fifteen minutes later.

He leaned over her shoulder slightly. "How else will you learn to be properly centered?"

"I guess I'll just have to suffer."

"Okay." He let go of her reluctantly. "As long as you understand you won't be the pro you would've been." He watched her land the ball in a lion's mouth, then peered at her closely. "Are you sure you haven't done this before?"

"No, but from the way things are going, maybe I should have," she allowed.

"You're a natural, all right." He grinned at her with respect, then smacked the ball over a giraffe and against the backboard. It rolled down next to the green.

"Close but no cigar."

He turned to grin at her. "You're more competitive than I imagined."

Anne was surprised that he liked that trait in her. Most men didn't. She rested her weight on her club. "I hear competition's a big thing in your family." She watched him closely.

John nodded and looked into her eyes. "Yeah. We all play sports and we all play to win." He hooked his club carelessly over his shoulder and stalked closer. The way he looked at her made her shiver. Though he wasn't touching her, she thought she knew how it would feel to be kissed by him.

"I had fun tonight," she admitted when they were finally back at her door again. He'd made her forget everything for a while. For the first time she could remember, she hadn't thought about the past; she hadn't thought about the future. All she'd thought about was the moment, John, how very good it felt to be with him and how good it might feel to kiss him someday.

"I'm glad," John said softly. "I was worried about you earlier."

"I know. But I feel better now."

He smiled, as though he, too, was wondering what it would be like to kiss her.

Feeling suddenly shy, Anne sighed. "But I know what I have to do now. I've got to go on with my life." She had to forget about her natural father. He didn't want her in his life. It was time she stopped lusting after the past. It was time she started living in the present, and spending time with John was a very pleasant way to start.

Chapter Seven

John kept an eye on the typewritten pages on his desk. He verbally ran through the speech while he hurriedly knotted his tie. After the fifth gaffe in a row, he swore in frustration. "Dammit, I'm never going to learn this commencement speech."

"I told you you were overcommitted this week," Lily said, looking equally exasperated. She handed him his suit coat.

"Gee, thanks for the support, Lil," John retorted dryly.

"Maybe if you practice while you're driving over to the high school," Lily suggested.

Normally John would have asked her to go with him and help him learn the speech en route, but he knew she had her hands full supervising the volunteers in the latest mailing. And there was no one else who could take her place. Her managerial skills were just too good.

John began the speech again and goofed again, royally. He swore under his breath. "You're right. I did take on too much. I'll never get this learned." He looked around for a volunteer and spotted Anne. She was covering her typewriter in the far corner of the outer room.

"Anne!" he called over the din of voices. "I need a favor. You're finished for the day, aren't you?"

"Yes." Anne looked at him, failing to hide her wariness. She had a lot to do back at her agency. Letters on Trong's behalf and follow-ups on other clients. "What kind of favor?"

"Nothing much," John reassured quickly. He hated her newfound caution where he was concerned. He also knew it was his fault. He should never have taken her to play miniature golf, or put his hands around her slim waist and aligned her willowy body with his. Hell, if he were perfectly honest, he knew he never should have gone over there Sunday night. It hadn't really been necessary. He'd just wanted to see her and find out what had been so important in Minneapolis.

Once he had gone to Anne's, he had been unable to leave. Cheering her up had led to physical teasing, increasingly intimate conversation and the growing sense that there could be something more between them. Since then, of course, he'd tried to maintain an officiously friendly but businesslike demeanor with her at the office. Rather than working to reassure her, his professional attitude seemed merely to have driven her farther away.

He approached her now. "How about riding over to the high school with me and prepping me on my commencement address for the graduating seniors?"

Anne stifled a groan. This wasn't part of her job, but he had been there for her when she needed him. "Sure," she said, promising herself she'd get to her work later that night, come hell or high water. Unable to resist teasing him, she said, "A quick study you're not, hmm?"

He gave her a droll look. "Don't start on me," he warned. "I've only had a zillion and one activities this week." He'd even met with an architect who had agreed to donate his services and design low-income housing.

"You're the one who insisted on accepting all those invitations," Lily sighed.

John turned to his office manager solicitously. "Next time stop me, okay?"

"I only wish I had that power," Lily volleyed back.

John paused. "Is it my imagination or is she a little tense?" he asked Anne when Lily had gone.

Anne thought Lily was a little tense. "I think we're all feeling a little frazzled, but it's no wonder, considering how crazy it's been around here."

"How are you doing on the party?" John asked, gathering the three pages of his speech and putting them in order.

"The caterers are all set, but we're still deciding on the menu. And some top country and rock acts have agreed to perform for free."

"You're kidding." John fell into step beside her. He held the outer door open, to let her pass. "How'd you manage that?"

Anne grinned. "I promised them lots of free publicity."

"Sounds like you've made a good start," John commented, admiration in his eyes.

Anne sighed. "There's still an awful lot to do, though." Both here and at home for Answers, Inc., she thought. However, she still owed him a favor and she'd do her best to oblige, even if it meant sitting through a dull ceremony.

"Have dinner with me," John urged hours later when the high school commencement had ended. "After making you sit through all that pomp and circumstance, feeding you is the least I can do."

Now that I'm working for his campaign, even temporarily, I shouldn't be going out with him socially, Anne told herself firmly. On the other hand, it was just one dinner, and she was famished. What could it hurt, especially when she knew her work for him would be finished in a few short weeks? "All right, thanks. Providing we make an early night of it." She still had work to do at home.

"No problem."

He chose a favorite gathering place of local politicians. Anne thought she knew why: they were less likely to be bothered. Still, her appearance with him would hit the local grapevine more quickly. Apparently he didn't care about that. She wasn't sure how she felt. Part of her was thrilled, the other part was all too wary. She knew from the talk in the office that he rarely went out with anyone more than a couple of times. That meant, in all likelihood, her time with him was limited. If he stayed true to form.

Once settled at their table, John watched the play of emotions on her face. "You seem in a pensive mood," he remarked softly. He wondered how much of her seeming restlessness had to do with him.

"I guess I am," Anne admitted. It hadn't been easy to accept his invitation. He was a very charming man. Women were attracted to him in droves. She hated to add herself to the pack. But that wasn't all that was bothering her. "Watching the seniors graduate brought back a lot of memories," she said. Even after his very full week, he looked negligently, arrogantly attractive in his usual windblown way.

He hesitated. "Good or bad?"

"A little of both, I suppose." She sat back in her chair. "It's exciting, moving on, but scary, too." It had made her realize she still didn't know what she was going to with her personal life. Would she ever marry or have children of her own? She wanted that. She wanted that with someone like John. Up until now, it hadn't seemed as though there was time. Now she was impatient to get on with it. "It's also a little daunting to realize I graduated over ten years ago."

"I know what you mean."

"That makes us both sound old."

"I guess, but I've always believed age was relative. After you reach adulthood, it's all a state of mind. We get wiser every year but not necessarily older, at least not in heart. You know what I mean?"

Anne nodded. In many ways she was the same girl she had been at eighteen. She still just wanted to know who she was and give and receive love unequivocably.

John smiled at her, thinking how pretty she looked in the soft glow of the candlelight, with her dark hair tied neatly back at her nape in a navy-blue bow that matched her dress. "Glad you're past all that?"

Anne thought about her high school days and the lack of dates. She hadn't been very popular, mainly because she hadn't tried to fit in with the girls. She'd had a lot more on her mind than shades of lipstick or the senior prom. The other girls hadn't. "Very glad," Anne confirmed, realizing that she wouldn't trade the past for the present, not for anything.

John had promised himself this wasn't a date, but he couldn't stop looking at her or feeling so attracted to her, especially now that they were away from the hustle and bustle of the office. He could tell by the spark of awareness in her eyes that she was wrestling with the same wealth of feeling he was. She wanted to be involved with him, even though she was fighting it.

"Where did you go to college?"

"University of New Hampshire, over in Durham. I was a psych major." Anne took a ladylike sip of her wine and wondered why their dinners of haddock au gratin were taking so long. "What about you?"

"Harvard, Harvard Law."

That figured, she thought. They were probably farther apart in life-style than she wanted to admit. "And before that?" she asked. She was aware she wanted to touch him even though she knew she shouldn't. She shouldn't be allowing him to get to her this way.

John smiled and clasped his hands loosely around his glass. "Before that, I was in prep school."

"Ah. Just like Tim," Anne said, trying not to notice how strong and tanned and capable his hands looked. She tried not to imagine how handsome he would have looked in a prep-school blazer and tie.

John poured them both a little more wine. "It's tradition for the men in the family. Prep school, then college or one of the academies, and then the military.

And then a life of politics, Anne thought, wondering what it would have felt like to have her whole life mapped out for her before she was even born. Was this part of what Tim was rebelling against? "Is Tim expected to go in the military, too?" She felt suffocated just thinking about it.

John put the bottle down slowly. "I know Frank would have liked it, but thus far Tim has no plans."

"How do you feel about that?"

John shrugged. "I think Tim would enjoy being in the military. I know I did, but he has to make up his own mind." Except when it came to finding his natural parents, Anne thought. And again she wondered why it was he was so opposed to helping Tim achieve his goals.

The rest of dinner passed too swiftly. They talked about everything and nothing and it was with deep regret that they finished their coffee and dessert. Around eleven, they headed to his car.

"Thanks for dinner," Anne said as they pulled up in front of the office building that housed his campaign headquarters.

"Thanks for helping me learn my speech. I couldn't have done it without you."

Anne accepted his gratitude with a brief nod and smile. John yearned to take her into his arms and kiss her, but feared such a move. This was going to be trickier than he thought. It was hard to have her work with him and get close to her at the same time. He didn't want Anne to feel he was harassing her and yet he wondered if he could wait until she'd left his employ before beginning a full-blown romance with her. He exercised his willpower and said good-night.

As Anne headed home, she thought about her first week on John's campaign. It had passed quickly; she'd divided her time between there and her office at home. But she wasn't sure she felt comfortable working on his staff. There was too much chaos, too many different people coming and going. She had to hand it to Lily, though. No matter what the crisis or problem, Lily had a solution. John depended on her heavily. Anne wasn't sure Lily really liked her, but she was glad John had Lily. With the crazy, demanding schedule he kept, he needed someone that efficient and flexible.

The light on her answering machine was blinking when Anne arrived home. When she pushed Play, a voice spoke in halting English. "Ms. Haynes? This is Son-ja Kim Hasegawa, Tim's natural mother. I receive your letter. I have come to Concord and I want very much to meet you."

It took a stunned but elated Anne less than ten minutes to drive over to Son-ja's hotel. The woman who opened the door was beautiful and richly dressed in a stunning emerald sheath. She was as cultured as Anne had hoped she would be. "It break my heart to have to give Tim up," Son-ja confided in halting English, over steaming cups of tea. "But I have no choice. My father, he say I no can keep my illegitimate child."

"What about Tim's father?" Anne asked. Son-ja had not gotten into that situation alone. Surely he should have been held accountable.

"Baby his responsibility, he agreed," Son-ja said, nodding emphatically. "That's why he take Tim back to the States."

"Wait a minute," Anne interrupted, not understanding. "Tim was adopted here by Frank and Gloria Westfield."

Jealousy and pain were both mirrored in Son-ja's dark eyes. "Yes. I know."

Anne sat in stunned silence, the cup of tea motionless on her lap. "Frank Westfield was Tim's natural father?" Anne's anger at John began to build.

Son-ja nodded solemnly. "Yes." She paused, confused. She peered at Anne closely. "You not know this?"

"No," Anne said. And this explained a lot. John, damn him, had worked hard to keep her in the dark. He didn't care that she was spending her hard-earned money and Tim's, searching for clues he had dishonestly and stealthily covered up. No wonder she'd had such trouble trying to find out anything specific about Tim's father. A cover-up had been implemented. No wonder John hadn't wanted her to investigate this for Tim! He had known what his brother had done, and supported the lies with more of his own. Hell, he had probably helped engineer the cover-up, all the while lying to her, to Tim, to Gloria and to the whole world.

Anne glanced at Son-ja, her own feelings in turmoil. She could never trust John again. And she was all too aware of how hurt and betrayed Tim could feel if this were ever disclosed. Because of John and Frank's dishonesty, they were all in a terrible jam. "Did Frank's wife know about Tim?"

"No." Son-ja shook her head sadly. "Frank tell my father Gloria never understand. You must understand. Frank was very good person. He love me but he also love his wife. I was very young. I loved him so. I wanted to believe everything be okay." She shook her head.

"But then you got pregnant," Anne said softly, sympathetically. "And your parents found out—"

"Yes. They very upset with me, tell me I no can keep Frank's baby and take me to convent where I stayed until my baby was born."

Anne imagined what that must have been like, and her heart went out to Son-ja. Why hadn't Frank been there for her, wife or no? "It must've been very hard to give him up," Anne said.

Son-ja nodded. "It break my heart. They never even let me see him." She shook her head and tears flowed from her eyes. Anne got up to give her a tissue and then waited patiently while Son-ja composed herself. As a result of the Westfield brothers' duplicity and the harsh, unforgiving attitude of Son-ja's family, they had all paid a terrible price.

"What happened afterward?" she asked.

"My father arrange marriage with a wealthy businessman from Japan. I go live there." She smiled through her tears. "I now have two children of my own. I have a good life."

"I'm glad," Anne said. It was reassuring to know one could go on after suffering such a terrible tragedy.

Son-ja put down her tea. She glanced at Anne shyly. "I want to meet Tim. That is why I come."

Anne wanted that, too. "I can arrange it," Anne said, already thinking ahead to John's reaction. It was bound to be very negative, but Tim's was bound to be jubilant. She gave Son-ja a cautioning look, "There's only one problem, Mrs. Hasegawa. And I'm sorry to say it's a big one."

"SO MY NATURAL father's dead," Tim said, during his emotional first meeting with his birth mother. Son-ja, Anne and Tim were cozily ensconced in Son-ja's luxurious hotel room.

Anne nodded. "Can't you find out anything more about him?" Tim pressed.

"No."

"Why not?"

Anne floundered. Furious at the position John had knowingly put her in, she yearned to confront him about what he'd done. Only her fear of further interference from him kept her from doing so. Right now, her concern had to be for her client and his mother, not for her own feelings of anger and betrayal. She and Son-ja had decided the night before it would be best to lie to Tim, rather than disillusion him completely about Frank, but Anne found lying very difficult. Averting her eyes, she focused briefly on the bouquet Tim had brought Son-ja.

"Why not?" Tim repeated.

"Because it wouldn't be fair to the privacy of his family."

"You mean he was married?" Tim frowned.

Anne wished fervently she had never opened this Pandora's box. She wished John were here, to tell the necessary lies. "Yes."

"Before or after he got involved with Son-ja?" Tim cast an inquiring look at his natural mother.

"Before," Son-ja said quietly. She paused, new tears beginning to glimmer in her eyes, "Tim, what we did was wrong. Now, I am older, I realize that."

And, Anne thought, John and Frank had probably realized it, too. But making a foolish mistake was one thing. Creating a web of never-ending lies to cover up that mistake was quite another.

"Are you telling me I was a mistake?" Tim asked his mother hoarsely.

Son-ja went to Tim and put her arms around him, hugging him close to her diminutive frame. "No. No, you are a beautiful boy." She lovingly ran her hands through the dark hair framing her son's face. "I am just saying I know what your father and I did was a sin because we were not married."

"Is that why you gave me up?" Tim asked, crying openly now. His pain was so great Anne had to turn away, lest she break down, too.

Son-ja nodded. "I did not want to. My family force me. But now I see you again, I realize it was best. You turned out fine, Tim. Very fine."

Tim swallowed hard. "All this time," he murmured, "I loved you. I didn't even know who you were and yet, in here—" he touched the region above his heart "—I loved you."

At that, Son-ja broke down completely. "I love you, too," she said. While Anne watched, tears streaming down her own face, Son-ja hugged her natural son very, very close.

ANNE was on her hands and knees, in front of the flower beds next to the house, when John dropped by. He looked angry with her, for her part in bringing Son-ja to Concord, and yet resigned to the situation, too. She knew how he felt. She was furious. Feeling grubby and disheveled in her old jeans and UNH sweatshirt, Anne glared at him resentfully when he hunkered down beside her.

"You could have told me, you know," Anne said, "instead of letting me spend all that time and energy looking. You could have just given me Son-ja's name and saved us all this trouble."

John's countenance was stony. "I promised my brother I wouldn't."

"And that made all the lies and your dishonesty all right?" Anne threw her spade blade-down, into the dirt.

"No," John said quietly, his lips white with strain. "It doesn't. But it doesn't mean I had a choice, either."

If John noticed Anne was close to tears of empathy and frustration, he gave no sign. "Tim told me he saw Son-ja," John said quietly.

Anne put down the gardenia she'd been planting and sat back, Indian-style, on the grass. "Did he tell Gloria?"

"That he met Son-ja? Yes. In fact, Gloria is having her over to the house tomorrow morning before she leaves for Tokyo."

Anne felt her breath stall in her chest. For Tim's sake, she wanted this to work out. "Then Gloria's not upset?"

John searched for words carefully. "I wouldn't say that exactly. It hurt her a lot, but she's dealing with it. Right now, that's about all one could ask."

Anne felt guilty for hurting Gloria, but she had no regrets about the happiness and relief Tim and his natural mother were now enjoying. Their particular situation, unlike her own, had turned out all right. Both were safe and happy and well. They knew they had much to be thankful for. With herself and Robert Ryan, that probably would never happen, no matter how much time passed or how much effort was made.

Never taking his eyes from her face, John moved to the porch steps and sat down opposite her. He said very, very casually, "Tim also said you wouldn't give him the name of his father."

"No." Uncomfortable with his steady scrutiny, Anne shifted her glance.

"Why not?" he pressed. Anne remained silent.

"You know, don't you," John guessed.

Now that they were finally being honest with each other, Anne saw no reason to pretend otherwise. "About Frank? Yes. Son-ja told me who Tim's father was."

John studied her intently. "Why didn't you tell Tim?"

Apparently this was some kind of character test, and John still hadn't decided quite how she fared. "I don't know." She shrugged, unable to adequately explain her action. Usually she was honest to a fault. She blew out a weary breath, feeling sadder and more disillusioned than ever. "I guess I just didn't see how it would help matters any. Neither did Son-ja. We both figured Tim had been hurt enough. To find out his own father and uncle had been too embarrassed to publicly acknowledge him would only hurt him more."

John struggled to contain his emotions. "Frank tried to do the right thing."

"Would Gloria really have left him if she'd known about Tim?"

"Probably. At least the way it was, Tim grew up with a mother and a father. He had roots, family. He didn't have to bear the emotional burden of being the reason for the breakup of Frank's marriage."

"Frank was responsible for that," Anne countered archly.

"You and I know that," John countered, "but it's doubtful Tim would've, then or now. He's a kid, and kids feel responsible for things like that."

Anne was silent, reluctantly admitting to herself that much was true. No matter what course Frank and John had taken, Tim would've been the one to suffer the most. In retrospect, right or wrong, she realized they'd done the best they could.

"So all these years you've known?" she asked finally, guessing what a heavy burden that must have been.

John nodded.

"Why did you cover for him?" she asked. How could he have gotten caught up in such treachery?

John gestured helplessly, at a loss to explain. "Because I idolized Frank," he said softly. "Because he was my older brother. Because he was in trouble and I wanted to help him, the way I want to help anyone who is in trouble."

Selfless to the end, Anne thought. She was unable to hold that against him, even though technically what he had done *had* been wrong.

"What about the rest of the family?" she asked. "Have they been told Tim's located his natural mother?"

John nodded. "They're taking it as well as could be expected, but Tim's disappointed he won't get to meet his natural father's family."

"Does he understand why not?"

John shook his head. "Not really. But he seems to accept the fact that neither you nor Son-ja will change your minds."

Anne went back to patting dirt around the newly transplanted gardenias, shoring them up so they'd grow straight and tall. "I wish we'd been able to think of a better story," she confessed, not looking at him directly.

"It's better to stick to the truth," John agreed. "Or at least as close to it as possible."

Anne's feelings were mixed. She still resented John's dishonesty with her, but she understood better than ever the mess he'd been in. Even now, there were no easy answers and no clear-cut path to take. The best any of them could manage would be to take it day by day.

"Are you angry with me?" John asked.

"A little," Anne admitted. Nevertheless, she felt better for the open way they had talked. She looked at him, searching his face. "Are you angry with *me?*"

He shrugged, his broad shoulders straining against the cotton of his shirt. "Not as much as I expected to be. I don't know." John gave her a level look. "Maybe meeting his mother and knowing he was loved from the very beginning will help Tim in the long run."

"I think that's something every child needs to know," she agreed softly. It was what she had needed from Robert Ryan and hadn't gotten.

"As for the rest of it, I guess we'll just have to see what happens."

JOHN WAS ON HIS WAY home, when he saw Tim parking across the street from the municipal tennis court. That in itself was not an oddity. Concord was a small city. Since John and Gloria owned homes in the same general area of town, he often passed Gloria or one of his teenage nieces or nephew on the street, particularly at night.

But he hadn't expected to see Tim out and about tonight, after the emotional day he'd had. Stranger still, John noted as he watched his nephew get out of the car, was the fact he had no racket and was dressed as if he were going out for the evening. John slowed down as he passed the courts, just in time to see his ex-wife Melinda move across a lighted area, toward Tim. She also had no racket.

Not wanting to infringe upon Tim's privacy, John kept driving, but by the time he'd gone another block, he knew he had to turn back. Something was going on. Ten to one, if his ambitious reporter of an ex-wife was involved, it wasn't good.

He parked down the street, and headed for the courts. He wasn't trying to eavesdrop, God knew, but their voices carried in the quiet night. "You've got to help me, Aunt Melinda. Dammit, I have a right to know who my natural father is, even if he's dead!"

"Tim, listen to me, I can't— John!" Melinda's face drained of color.

Tim whirled to face John, looking angry and upset. "What are you doing here?"

John struggled to remain calm. It was this kind of reaction he had been fearing and waiting for all along.

He should have known it would come. "What's going on?" he asked them both casually.

Tim's face grew sullen. He looked at Melinda, as if daring her to tell on him. She didn't. "Think about what I said, Aunt Melinda. *Please*. If you don't help me—" he shot a miserable, accusing look at John "—I don't know who will." He brushed past.

John was left facing Melinda. Odd, he thought, that they could have been married for five years. As he faced her now, a scant two years later, he felt so little of what he had then. "I'm sorry, John." Melinda dug her toe into the court beneath her feet. "He called me and insisted we meet."

John didn't blame her. He knew if she hadn't gone, Tim would have just turned to someone else. "He told you about finding his real mother?" John felt uneasy. The information was like a lit grenade in an election year, and Melinda knew it as well as he did.

"And about not finding his father," Melinda admitted, casting John a vaguely hurt, quizzical look. "He thinks you're all lying to him, covering up again. Including Anne Haynes." She paused a heartbeat. "Is it true?"

Without warning, John wanted to protect Anne. Unable to answer Melinda's question honestly, John phrased one of his own, one he knew Melinda couldn't answer. "Why would Anne want to lie to Tim?"

Melinda regarded him with dogged curiosity. "That's what I want you to tell me."

John was again struck by how little he had really shared with Melinda. It amazed him that he'd been able to tell Anne about the most intimate details of his life in the short time they'd known each other. Maybe it was the fact that Anne was searching for answers, too. And maybe that had nothing to do with it. Maybe it was just Anne, the fact that when she looked at him he felt the depth and warmth of her inner compassion.

"Who's Tim's father?" Melinda asked.

"How would I know?"

Melinda didn't drop her gaze. "Perhaps because Frank probably knew. And the two of you shared a lot. It may even have been a friend of his. Now wouldn't *that* be something."

"Melinda, please—"

She held up both hands. "We're not married anymore, John. I don't owe you any favors."

He advanced on her roughly, aware his patience was at an end. "I'm asking for one anyway."

"No," Melinda cut him off stubbornly.

"Whatever happened with Tim's mother is private, Melinda."

"Are you saying this because you're campaigning?" she asked sweetly. Her tone reminded him how much she had hated the demands of political life, especially in the end.

John folded his arms. "I'm saying it because it's true."

"The truth has a way of coming out, you know," she warned.

"Not if we don't want it to be revealed, it won't." He reached out to touch her arm imploringly. "Please, Melinda. Don't open this can of worms."

Shrugging out from under his light grasp, Melinda ran a hand through her wavy red hair. "You know what you're asking of me. My career practically died while I was married to you. It was all I could do to get it jump-started again. Something like this would be a fabulous coup."

"I know that. Please, Melinda. I'll give you any other kind of interview you want, for any publication. Just do my family a favor and let this one go."

Melinda sighed reluctantly, finally bowing to his pressure, for old time's sake. "All right, John. You win, as usual. I'll let it go." Against her wishes, her look seemed to say.

"Thanks," John said. "I appreciate it."

Melinda merely looked at him sourly and shook her head in admonition. "I just keep wishing life were easier, you know?" she said as they walked in tandem to the car.

John nodded. He wished that, too, all the time, but it wasn't. "I know."

Chapter Eight

"You want me to go with you to your family compound on Lake Winnipesaukee?" Anne asked John the following week. She was amazed he would ask her to accompany him to such an intimate, family-oriented event. Not that they hadn't spent time together. They'd both stayed late to go over the final guest list for the July Fourth celebration. They'd both met with the fire marshal to ensure the fireworks they'd be using were safe. This morning, she'd talked to him briefly about the advisability of securing tents for the lawn, in case it rained.

"Yeah. As friends." John watched her check the address on the master guest list. "We had fun playing putt-putt together, didn't we?" he persisted.

"Yes," she admitted shyly, not looking at him, "we did." That didn't mean they should date when she was working with him so closely. It hadn't mattered that there were scores of people around them both, or that she saw him for only a short time every day. She was increasingly aware of John on a man-woman level, and she suspected from the intent way he looked at her that he felt the same.

"Well?"

"Well, I don't know anyone," she said lamely.

"You know Tim and Gloria," John pointed out equably.

"Both of whom are probably mad at me right now," Anne countered.

John shrugged, unconcerned. "They'll get over it. And, as for Tim, he should be grateful to you." Anne noticed John didn't mention Gloria again. "Besides, it'll give you a chance to check out the layout of the house and grounds in person. Wouldn't you like to see where the July Fourth party is going to be held?"

Anne had to admit that would help her plan the party more efficiently.

"Come on," John continued. "What do you say? Everyone and their dog is going to be there."

Anne laughed. "Is that a roundabout way of getting me not to make too much of this invitation?" In the foreground she saw Lily in the outer office, working with one of the volunteers.

"If I say yes, will that get you to come?" John teased, his full attention still centered on her.

It would help, Anne thought. Heaven help her, she didn't want to fall in love with this charming man, not knowing that what they wanted and expected out of life was so very different. "I've read about the Westfield family gatherings," Anne responded. Kennedy-esque in nature, the Westfield family parties featured sailing, football on the lawn, tennis, lots of children and dogs and chaos.

Never comfortable among strangers, the idea of attending a party like that filled Anne with fear. And yet at the same time she longed to go with John. She wanted to spend some fun time alone with him, the kind they'd had when they played putt-putt. She wanted to meet his uncles, aunts, and cousins. She wanted to meet those close to him and get some sense of his early life. And yet she was also very afraid that those close to him would disapprove of her, the way she sometimes felt Lily secretly did. "Will your parents be there?" she asked.

"No," John said. "They're still in Belgium, with the American embassy." He paused, studying the mixed emotions on her face. "Disappointed?"

Relieved would be more like it, Anne thought. John's father, in particular, was supposed to be formidable, wanting only the very best for his sons. She feared under the best of circumstances she wouldn't pass muster with him. And yet a part of her did want to meet John's parents, if only to get some sense of him. "A little," she admitted.

John was quick to reassure her. "Well, don't fret about it. They'll be back after the New Year. You can meet them then."

If we're still going out by then, Anne thought. Considering his reputation as a man about town, that probably wouldn't be the case.

John saw she was still considering his invitation. "Cross my heart, I promise." He drew an X across his chest. "No one will throw you in the pool. And you don't have to do anything you don't want to do."

He's not going to let me say no, she thought. He'll stay here and persuade me to do what he wants if it takes all night.

"What time?"

John grinned, victorious. "I'll pick you up at eight Saturday morning."

Fortunately Anne was so busy the rest of the week, juggling her work at Answers, Inc. and her work for John that she had little time to agonize over her decision. Only on Friday did she begin to dwell on it again, wondering what would be expected of her socially.

"What's the dress for this party on Saturday?" Anne asked Lily over lunch, when she learned Lily was driving up to the lake, too.

"Casual. You can wear anything you want, although I'd stay away from anything too casual, like cutoffs or halters," Lily said helpfully. "But really, anything cotton and coordinated will do."

Contemplating her wardrobe, Anne tensed.

"Relax. You really have nothing to worry about. Since I've been working for John, I've been to lots of Westfield parties up at Lake Winnipesaukee. At least five or six a year. They always invite the staff. It's no big deal."

Lily's airy attitude made Anne feel both better and worse. "Did you ever drive out with John?" Anne asked.

Lily paused, her expression becoming unreadable. "Yeah, I did," she said softly. She looked suddenly older than her twenty-three years. "A couple of times, right after his divorce."

"But not since," Anne ascertained, feeling her hopes that this was the start of something special between herself and John die.

"John always tries to make new staffers welcome. Once you are, well, then you're on your own."

"Oh," Anne said, feeling more disappointed and apprehensive than ever.

"Cheer up," Lily said, glancing at Anne's downcast expression. "There'll be so many people there, you probably won't have to deal with John's ex-wife, Melinda, at least not one-on-one, like you did at that thousand-dollar-a-plate dinner John took you to."

Despair welled in Anne. "Melinda'll be at this party, too?" she asked. She felt as though she wanted to go home, climb into bed, and pull the covers over her head. This was getting worse and worse!

Lily shrugged, seeing nothing to get excited about. "Probably so. You know what they say, once a Westfield, always a Westfield. But Melinda loves to sail, so, luckily for all of us, she'll be off with some of the cousins doing that most of the day."

By the time John picked Anne up Saturday morning, she fervently regretted ever accepting his invitation. "You feeling okay?" he asked as they walked out to the car. "You look a little pale."

"I was up late last night," Anne said, hoping the jaunty navy-and-white sailor top, matching slacks, and white cotton deck shoes were appropriate for the activities of the day.

He looked crisp and neat himself in khaki shorts and a bright teal-blue polo shirt and deck shoes. "My work or yours?"

"Mine. I've kind of fallen behind." The truth was she hadn't been able to accomplish much on Trong's case since she'd cut back to half time at the agency. But that was going to change after the Fourth, she told herself determinedly. She'd have enough money saved up to work at Answers, Inc. full-time. She would no longer have to worry about John's family, or fitting in, or how he'd feel if the Westfields couldn't accept her.

Despite all she'd seen and read over the years, Anne was not prepared for the luxuriousness and grandeur of the Westfield compound. The sprawling white-brick mansion was spread out across one hundred acres of prime lakefront, and surrounded by a twelve-foot chain-link privacy fence. Late model cars, Jeeps and even a few dune buggies were parked at odd angles all along the long, winding, tree-lined driveway. Behind the house, she could see several tennis courts, a huge swimming pool, cabana and a covered latticework pavilion.

In the distance, children and animals alike frolicked along the private beach that stretched as far as the eye could see. Down near the private marina, teenagers and adults manned gaily colored sailboats and several small speedboats that pulled people on water skis. The Westfields' idea of fun looked like a lot of work, Anne thought, and not at all the tranquilizing balm she had been promised. On the other hand, seeing the place in person, it was easy to imagine how wonderful the July Fourth party could be, with festive streamers on the lawn, sparklers and games for the children, fireworks, food and live music.

"Relax," John said. They got out of his car and prepared to join the others. "You'll do fine." And to make sure she did, he showed her around personally, introducing her to a dizzying number of people, all of whom were related, either by blood, marriage, work or friendship, to members of the energetic, civic-minded Westfield clan.

Most imposing of all, was the matriarch of the large, political family, John's grandmother, Margaret Westfield. Nearly eighty, she dropped the baby booties she had been knitting into her lap, slid her jewel-rimmed bifocals down to the end of her slim, patrician nose and looked Anne up and down in a deftly appraising way that made Anne's stomach quiver. "Hello, dear," she said pleasantly in a voice that was television-announcer-perfect.

"Hello, Mrs. Westfield." Anne had to resist the urge to curtsy, so strong was her feeling she was in the presence of royalty.

"John, Lily was looking for you earlier." Margaret nodded in the direction of Lily and picked up her knitting again. "Something about a problem with next week's agenda." She smiled at him warmly, all the love she felt for him showing plainly on her elegant wrinkled face. "You run along and find her and get that straightened out. Meanwhile, Anne can stay here with me." She patted the wooden rocker beside her. "It'll give us a chance to get acquainted."

John looked at Anne, hoping it was all right with her.

"It's okay," she lied, telling herself everything was going to be fine. "I'll catch up with you later," she promised.

John nodded, looking relieved his grandmother, with her imposing but loving manner, hadn't managed to spook Anne yet. "I'll be back in a jiff."

Margaret turned to Anne the moment John ran off. She focused her sole attention on Anne. "So, Anne, you love politics, too, I presume."

Anne dearly wished she could say she did, but if anything, the past weeks had shown her she was not cut out for political life. She agreed with John's politics and admired his tenacity, positive spirit, and civic-mindedness, but the idea of campaigning city to city for months at a time boggled her mind. She couldn't tell Margaret Westfield that, without risking blatant disapproval, so Anne searched her mind for something nice to say. Finally she untied her tongue long enough to say, "Well, I'm learning a lot. There's a lot more to this campaigning business than I ever imagined. And John's been very good to me, giving me a temporary job."

Margaret knew horse manure when she heard it. She also realized quickly what Anne hadn't said, that she loved the highs and lows of politics every bit as much as John. Her patrician posture got a little stiffer. "So you don't plan to stay on after you finish planning the party for the Fourth—not even as a volunteer?"

"No," she forced a trembling smile, feeling more nervous than ever. So this was the hot seat. "I have my own work."

"Yes," Margaret said, with arch disapproval, "I heard." She paused, and began to knit vigorously, despite hands that looked quite arthritic. "I suppose you already know his romantic history." She knitted faster and faster.

With difficulty, Anne tore her eyes from the superb stitchery in progress. "I beg your pardon?" She looked at Margaret with a bewildered expression.

Margaret's chin lifted. Her eyes bore into Anne's. "I am speaking of the fact John already had one wife who let him down by not being as passionately interested in politics and this family as he was." She underlined her words with unmitigated warning. "I hope whoever John gets involved with next understands how important both are to him and feels the same."

"It'd be hard not to realize that," Anne said, feeling as if she'd just been grilled alive by the elegant softspoken lady. "John makes no secret of his ambition. He's running for governor, after all."

Margaret's shrewd gaze narrowed as she continued to knit swiftly. "John needs a *wife* who is up to the demands that are put upon the first lady of this state. Someone who is comfortable entertaining visiting dignitaries, who knows protocol, someone who is willing to give up her own career and identity and immerse herself in that of her husband's."

No wonder Melinda had found her life with him intolerable, Anne thought. There weren't many women in this day and age who could happily submerge themselves so thoroughly in their husbands' careers. Never mind be forced into it by the husband's extended family. "It's a large price to pay," Anne said candidly, meeting the older woman's gaze and letting her know she would not be pressured so easily.

"Yes, it is," Margaret agreed flatly. "And it's also a price that will have to be paid. John's divorce was scandal enough. He can't afford another mistake."

There was no disguising Margaret's intent. She wanted to let Anne know she wasn't right for John. Hearing the truth in what she said and the forewarning, Anne felt her face flame.

John returned in time to hear his grandmother mention his divorce. To his credit, he didn't look any happier than Anne felt about the impromptu lecture session. "Hey, enough about my love life," he interjected lightly. He glanced at Anne affectionately, gave her a hand up from her seat, tightened his arm possessively around her waist and drew her in close to his side. "You're probably boring this lady to tears, Gran." John's politely uttered words were laced with double meaning: they told his grandmother to lay off.

Margaret smiled. "I don't think I was boring her," she countered, just as deliberately, not backing down one iota. "In fact, Anne seemed quite interested in all I had to say."

John nodded, looking unconvinced. "I'll bet," he said dryly.

"Don't let her get to you," John advised moments later, after he'd politely excused the two of them. He and Anne walked across the lawn. The arm he had circled loosely around her waist tightened. "Gran's bark is worse than her bite."

Anne wished she could be sure of that. "She didn't scare me." Nevertheless, she was glad John was holding on to her so firmly. After the silk-edged confrontation with Margaret, her legs felt none too steady.

"Good. Because there's probably no stopping her. And it's not just that she feels intensely protective of her family. At seventy-nine, Gran feels entitled to speak her mind."

She'd done that all right, Anne thought. "Yes, well, at my ripe old age, I feel the same way," she bantered back mildly. She cast him a rueful glance. "I'm afraid I didn't handle it as well as I could have."

"Why? What'd you say?" He stopped walking and turned her to face him. They were sheltered by a neat hedge, bordered with blooming tulips. Anne noticed how green his eyes looked today and how glossy, soft, and windblown his medium-brown hair seemed. She longed to touch it.

"I said I didn't think a woman should have to give up her own hard-won career and identity simply because her husband happened to be a politician."

John grimaced as if in pain, then said dryly, "I bet that went over like a lead balloon."

Anne spread her hands nonchalantly, giddily aware John wasn't angry with her, just a little ticked off at his grandmother for putting her in such a spot.

He pursed his delectably full lips and prodded, "Go on."

"Yes, well . . . I said it about that time she informed me you couldn't afford any more romantic mistakes." She thinks I'm one of them, Anne added silently, depressed once again.

"Yeah, I heard that much of it," John said regretfully. He rested both hands lightly on her shoulders, his palms cupping her with warmth. His eyes held hers. "For what it's worth, I don't think you're a mistake. Gran won't, either," he predicted with his usual optimism, "when she gets to know you."

Anne wished fervently that were so. Unfortunately she did not have John's confidence, not about his family or anything else it seemed. The two of them resumed walking toward the house. "She was also disappointed that I don't plan to keep working for your campaign after the Fourth."

John looked as if he shared that sentiment with his grandmother. "I understand you have your own work."

"It's not that I won't vote for you. I will." She knew him well enough now to realize he'd make an excellent governor. She wanted him to understand. "But politics is not my cup of tea. And I can't and won't pretend it is. I just don't have the enthusiasm or aptitude for it. For instance, I could never work the crowds the way you do."

"Don't sell yourself short," John said gruffly, reaching over to squeeze her hand. "You're very persuasive when you're passionate about something. You'd be an ace politician. You just have to find your niche. Mrs. Reagan had her campaign against drugs.

Mrs. Bush fights illiteracy. And both did damn fine jobs. Why? Because they believed in what they were doing. If you were ever in a position to do the same, I have no doubt you'd tackle the job with the same verve and initiative as those two women."

Anne smiled, liking the company he put her in. "Keep talking," she teased, wishing fervently she could believe in herself the way he believed in her, from the depths of his soul. "I think some of that good old Westfield confidence is starting to rub off on me."

"Good," John said firmly, squeezing her hand. "Because you should be confident, Anne. You have a lot going for you and—"

"Uncle John!" Three teenage girls in shorts and halter tops breathlessly interrupted. "They need you over at the tennis courts! The men's tournament is starting and you're up first!"

John shot Anne an apologetic glance, then introduced her to Gloria's three daughters, Susie, Hope and Betsy. Just that quickly, he was ready to abandon her, it seemed. He excused himself, adding warmly, "Feel free to make yourself at home."

At home, here? Anne thought, gulping inwardly. Walking around the grounds with her arm tucked beneath his was one thing. Walking around alone was quite another. She didn't want to risk another run-in with his grandmother, and she feared everyone else in his close-knit clan might be just as brutally protective of him. But John appeared to think she was in no danger, immediate or otherwise.

"Don't worry, we'll entertain her!" sixteen-year-old Susie, the eldest and prettiest of the three girls, promised.

Satisfied that he was leaving her in good hands, John dashed off to join the crowd of men waiting for him at the courts. Anne watched him go. It was childish but she was unable to help it. She felt vaguely disgruntled, abandoned and lonely already.

"So is it serious between you and Uncle John?" Betsy, the athletic thirteen-year-old, asked mischievously, pushing forward until she stood toe to toe with Anne.

"Get real!" fourteen-year-old Hope said, elbowing her baby sister aside. High-strung and studious-looking, Hope obviously had little tolerance for her youngest sister's verbal faux pas.

"I don't see why not." Betsy defended herself energetically, though her sparkling expression said she knew full well why Anne probably wouldn't answer.

"I do!" Susie said with all the know-it-all flair of an oldest sibling. She flung her gorgeous long brown hair out of her face. "She probably doesn't want it all over the state that they're having a hot romance. That's private," she explained to her younger sisters.

"I'm not having a hot romance," Anne defended herself, stepping back apace from the lively trio. *Not yet, anyway.* She couldn't deny the possibility crossed her mind with increasing frequency.

All three girls giggled at once in response to Anne's denial. "Look!" Betsy said to Susie, delighted, "you made her blush!"

Hope elbowed Betsy. "You're going to get us all in trouble!" she hissed. "If Mom hears us—you know how she feels about us embarrassing Uncle John's—er—uh, friends!"

There they went again, Anne thought with an inward sigh, talking about John's girlfriends, plural.

"Hope's right!" Susie elbowed Betsy. "Apologize—right now!"

"Oh, all right, all right!" Betsy said, sulking. She peered at Anne closely and said, "You're not mad at us, are you?"

Anne shook her head. She knew the lively group of girls meant no harm. "No."

Without warning, Gloria joined the group. Looking fragile and cool, she lightly touched the shoulders of all three of her daughters, gently and wordlessly getting their attention, then murmured, "Girls, I think you're needed down at the beach, to look out for some of your younger cousins."

"Okay, Mom!"

Anne could tell Tim's mother was furious with her for finding Tim's natural mother and bringing about their emotion-packed reunion. This was something else she didn't want to face. She knew she had done what was right for Tim, but she'd had enough experience with her own parents' feelings to realize Gloria would never agree with her. "About Son-ja—"

"She seems like a lovely woman," Gloria allowed stiffly, still giving Anne a dagger-filled look. "Tim was quite taken with her," she finished in a low, brittle tone.

And Gloria was very hurt and very threatened. "Too bad you couldn't have found his father, too, to make his defection complete," Gloria murmured. With tears in her eyes, she stalked off to join her girls.

Anne sagged with relief and leaned up against a nearby tree. She'd only been here an hour and already she felt as if she'd just run a twenty-six-mile marathon. How would she manage to make it through the entire day? Especially with John *not* by her side?

"Excuse me, have you seen Melinda Parker?" a pleasant-looking woman asked Anne. She held out her hand. "By the way, I'm Francine Westfield Baker, John's cousin on his father's side. I'm sorry we haven't been introduced. You're his date, aren't you?"

"Yes," Anne thought, bracing herself for endless speculation about the nature of her relationship with the handsome politician.

"Then you probably know Melinda—" Francine continued.

"Yes."

Francine frowned. "She was supposed to drive out early this morning to make the potato salad for the evening meal and she hasn't shown up yet, and I've got my hands full." She snapped her fingers. "Hey, I don't suppose you'd agree to pitch in? It'd be easy, I swear. The potatoes and eggs are already cooked."

Getting away from the throngs of Westfields peppering the lawn sounded like heaven. Plus, Anne knew how fast time could go when she was busy. Hiding out in the kitchen sounded like a great idea. "Sure, I'd be glad to help."

Anne was deposited in the kitchen in front of two stainless-steel restaurant-sized salad dishes. There was a huge mound of potatoes, at least seventy-five, two dozen hard-boiled eggs, two bundles of celery, a dozen onions, and a large bottle of premixed, preseasoned dressing. Anne began to have her doubts. In theory, her chore seemed elementary enough. All she had to do was slice, dice and mix, but the unsettling fact was she'd never prepared anything for such a large crowd before.

Too late, Francine was gone, and there was no one else in the kitchen, save children running in and out now and then to help themselves to Popsicles or glasses of Kool-Aid.

Telling herself firmly she could do this simple task and do it well, Anne began peeling the cooked potatoes. The aroma of charcoal wafted in through the open windows. Music blared on the lawn. Voices laughed and called to one another. She felt lonely and as isolated as hell.

By the time she'd finished the first dozen potatoes, however, another of John's cousins had come in to work on the fruit salad. Soon after that, Francine was back, instructing someone else to begin the baked beans. Gloria's three daughters came in to shuck corn. Lily and Gloria snapped green beans.

Contentment filled Anne as she worked and talked, and the capable Francine orchestrated it all, directing young men in shorts and tank tops to carry the large platters of meat out to the grills their fathers were now manning. Soon the smell of roasting weiners, hamburgers, turkey and chicken filled the charcoal-scented air. Under Francine's capable direction, the dozen and a half picnic tables on the lawn were dragged together and covered with red-checkered cloths. It was time to bring out the food.

"Okay," Francine said, stopping before the brimming bowls of salad that had, Anne thought, admiring her handiwork, turned out very nicely. "Which one contains onion and which doesn't?"

Anne blinked, hoping she hadn't heard right, and then knew from the look on Francine's face she had. "I—put onion in all the potato salad," Anne heard herself saying meekly.

Francine recovered quickly. "I forgot to tell you, didn't I?" John's cousin asked softly, more distressed with herself than with Anne. "Well, it's about time that tradition was broken, anyway. We'll all eat onion today," she said firmly, waving off the mistake. "It doesn't matter."

Nevertheless, Anne felt a little crushed and ineffective. And those feelings increased as the complaints about her mistake were heard again and again. It didn't matter that they were promptly shushed by the adults who were in the know about the reason for the mistake. The fact was Anne had failed. Again.

She got through the meal without showing her distress, but when it finally came time for dessert, she knew she couldn't manage another moment. Waiting until John went in to help bring out the dizzying array of cakes, pies, and cookies, she slipped off through the trees and moved in the falling darkness toward the beach.

She told herself she just needed a moment alone, away from all the chaos, noise and reminders of her mistake. But as each moment passed, it got harder and harder to think about going back. It was quiet. Lonely, but safe. Down here, she couldn't draw attention to herself again in a negative way.

An hour later, John found her in a canvas beach chair that she'd dragged up next to the trees. "There you are," he said, without the least bit of negative judgment in his low, sexy tone.

Looking up, she saw he had a plate with a piece of chocolate cake; a steaming cup of coffee was in his hand. Although he was trying his best to hide it, he looked a little hurt by her admittedly childish disappearing act, and she felt guilty for running off and leaving him without a word.

She expected him to be angry with her, or disillusioned by her lack of adaptability, but his demeanor was tender and kind. He took the low-slung beach chair closest to her. "You missed dessert," he began gently as he handed her the plate and cup. "So I brought you some."

His kindness only made her feel more guilty. "You didn't have to do that," she said, embarrassed.

"Sure I did," he said easily. He wrapped her stiff hands around the steaming mug. "The chocolate hazelnut torte is great. You've got to try it."

Anne took the plate and set it on her lap. Before she could bring herself to try a bite, he said, "Francine told me about the potato salad. She wants you to know she feels awful. She'll tell you so herself, when you go back up with the others."

That was the whole point, Anne didn't *want* to go back. She didn't want to be where she didn't fit in. It was just too painful. It reminded her too much of the past.

Embarrassed and restless, Anne stood, put her dishes in her chair and paced to the water's edge. John followed her. "Francine doesn't need to apologize to me, John. It was my mistake," she said. She slipped her hands deep into the pockets of her slacks. "I should have asked her how she wanted the salads fixed." But she hadn't. Like so many times before, Anne had just assumed and assumed wrong.

He moved behind her, his voice as easy and relaxed as his tall frame. "Don't be so hard on yourself, Anne. The way things were laid out, it was a natural assumption—"

Anne didn't suffer fools gladly, and she didn't like those who did, even when they were trying to make her feel better. "There were two bowls, John." *And plenty of time to ask for instruction, if she'd so chosen. She hadn't.*

"And enough potatoes and onions to fill both," John countered reasonably. He turned so the wind off the lake was blowing into his face.

Anne turned to face him and found herself locked in a stalemate with John. She stared at him wordlessly, knowing that he thought she was being silly and knowing she probably was. He wanted her to forgive herself and just enjoy what remained of the evening with his family, but as much as she wanted to let it go, too, she simply couldn't. It was too reminiscent of her inability to ever really fit in, the way a native-born American would.

"Why are you being so hard on yourself?" When she didn't answer, he put his hands on her shoulders and forced her to face him squarely. Exasperation crept into his low tone. "It really wasn't a big deal, Anne. You don't need to make this into an international crisis."

She ducked her head, her eyes filling with tears caused by the strain of the day. The grilling by his family and having to make herself at home among a crowd of gregarious strangers in a strange place had been difficult. His life was so unlike her own. For the millionth time, she wondered what she was doing there with him. Anne had some idea now why Melinda had found it so hard to become a Westfield. There was just so much to learn, so much required. You were supposed to be lively, good at sports, charming and quick to join in. You were supposed to be intuitive and helpful and above all, remarkably resilient. It would have been difficult for anyone.

"No one wants you to feel bad," John continued reiterating.

She knew that. She also knew some things were easier said than done. "You don't understand," she said. "Things like this happen to me all the time. I try to blend in, and the more I try, the more I stand apart." And she hated that. All she had ever wanted was to belong.

He looked at her, all the compassion in his heart revealed in his low, soft tone and gentle touch. "We're not talking about potato salad now, are we?" With a low oath about her stupid pride, he dragged her into his arms. She turned her head away from him. Refusing to let her go, he held her anyway, his arms warm and strong around her.

"We'd better go back," Anne finally said.

"I'm in no hurry. Besides, I wanted you to try this cake, remember?" He got her dessert, forked up a mouthful and held it to her lips.

Anne hadn't been fussed over so much for years. She let him slip the fork past her lips. The gooey, rich dessert melted on her tongue, fulfilling his every promise of a delectable treat.

"You like it?" John asked, his eagerness to please her as endearing as his need to somehow save her with his presence.

Anne nodded, finding it suddenly very hard to swallow when he was looking at her so intently. "Heaven."

John smiled and put the plate aside. "No," he corrected romantically, taking her back into his arms. "*This* is heaven."

He was right, Anne thought dizzily seconds later as his mouth covered hers in a tender, searing kiss. This was heaven. He released her slowly, by degrees. "Still want to go back?" he whispered throatily, "Or are you game for a little stroll down the beach?"

Home Free

She wanted to go with him more than she could say. A deeply ingrained sense of propriety, however, made her insist, "Your family—"

John grinned. "That's the good thing about a family my size. We'll never be missed. Besides, you look like you need time out, and to be honest, Annie, so do I. This endless socializing can get very wearying, even for us Westfields."

For the next few minutes, they walked contentedly in the moonlight that reflected off the surface of the lake. The sounds of the party grew more and more distant. The feel of her hand clasped firmly in his felt more and more natural. "Is this the end of your property?" Anne asked, trying hard to mask her letdown. She glanced at the trees lining the shore and noticed they arrowed down to a rocky U-shaped cove some eight feet high. They were truly at a dead end.

"Yes," John said. He pulled her around by the shoulders, clasped her warmly and brought her to him.

She'd felt vaguely out of place all day, but not now. One second in his arms and she knew she was home. One second of his kiss and she knew this man, this time, was different. She knew she was everything he wanted her to be. And in turn, he was all she had ever dreamed of. He made her forget time and place. She didn't need to think, worry or agonize. She was aware only of his long, drugging kisses and her own sighs. She felt the hardness of his thighs pressed against hers, and higher still, the insistent and evocative male pressure of his desire. He wanted her, wanted her desperately, and as she wreathed her arms tightly around his neck, she wanted him. And she wasn't afraid to show him.

When they finally drew apart, they heard high-pitched teenage laughter moving toward them. "So much for privacy," John murmured reluctantly, drawing back.

He looked, Anne thought, much as she guessed she did. His hair was tousled by the wind and her roaming fingers; his lips were still damp and swollen with passion.

Slowly, his eyes still holding hers and loving hers, John released her. "I guess we weren't the only ones with this idea," he murmured in wry satisfaction. Both of them combed their fingers through their hair, trying to restore some semblance of order.

"I guess not," Anne said, trying not to sound too disappointed.

"We better get back," he said, looking and sounding as let down about the untimely end of their tryst as she felt.

Anne nodded. They didn't want to get caught necking by Gloria's kids, but she'd never felt less like returning to a party in her life.

Chapter Nine

John added milk and sugar to his Wheaties and carried the bowl into the living room for a leisurely Sunday morning breakfast. A rerun of *Midway,* one of his all-time favorite movies, was playing on HBO, but all he could think about was Anne. Funny, how he took the circus his family called a "picnic" for granted. He'd grown up so used to chaos and people that he was able to feel at home anywhere. The same wasn't true for Anne. Although she'd tried to put on a brave and valiant front, she had been out of her element the previous day.

He sighed, remembering how he had panicked when he'd first found her missing. Luckily his niece Betsy had spotted her heading toward the beach. So he'd known just where to look.

Of course, maybe Anne's uneasiness around his family was to be expected. The rambunctious, gregarious Westfield clan was a lot for anyone to take, and that went double for someone with Anne's background. The rigors of politics and the harsh scrutiny of the press and public would be very hard on someone like Anne. She'd had a hard enough time dealing with his family, Gran especially, and yet strangely enough, none of that mattered to him. Maybe because kissing her and holding her in his arms had felt so right. He had wanted to erase the sadness and uncertainty in her eyes and let her know she belonged with him. And for a while he had. If they hadn't been on the beach...if they hadn't been interrupted...she would probably still be with him right now. He sighed.

The doorbell rang. Putting his cereal aside, he answered it and was surprised to see Melinda standing on his doorstep. "What's up?" he asked curiously, taking in her grim, reluctant expression.

Melinda tensed. "May I come in?" Her voice was low, urgent. "I need to talk to you."

"Sure." His edginess increasing, John ushered his ex-wife into the living room. "We missed you at the picnic yesterday," he commented casually.

"I was working."

"Saturday evening, too?" No wonder she looked so tired. "Want some Wheaties? A cup of coffee?"

"No thanks. John—" Melinda sighed. "Don't hate me for this," she said. She looked as though this was absolutely the last place on earth she wanted to be. "I had to do it."

John wasn't sure what she was trying to tell him. He only knew it wasn't good, not by a long shot. A combination of irritation and fear made him snap impatiently, "Had to do what?"

Her face paled even more at his lack of compassion. "The story," she whispered, her mouth trembling. "On Frank. And Tim."

There was only one reason she would have linked those two names together that way. John reacted as if he'd been sucker-punched in the gut. The air left his lungs in one big whoosh. His abdomen cramped with sudden, severe pain. It was all he could do to keep up the charade his brother Frank had insisted on. "What are you talking about?"

Melinda's blunt gaze met his. "You know what I'm talking about," she said quietly. The regret on her face told him she knew damn well how traitorously she had just betrayed him and his entire family.

Melinda continued, "And unless I miss my guess, that's exactly why you've been working so hard to keep Tim from finding out. Because you knew Tim was Frank's illegitimate child."

John swallowed. This information would have been dangerous in any hands. In the care of his career-minded ex-wife, it was doubly so. "How did you find out?" he asked, his fear slowly being replaced by anger. Melinda knew how much this would hurt Tim, Gloria and the girls better than anyone. She had persisted, for her own gain.

"I did some digging. It wasn't all that hard."

For someone with Melinda's intellect and determination, probably not, John thought grudgingly. Still, he felt she owed him some loyalty. The Westfields had taken her in and made her one of them. Was this how she repaid them? Fighting to hold on to his soaring temper, he lifted his brow. "Even after I asked you not to?"

Melinda tightened her jaw defensively. "Tim was not going to let it go. He was ready to approach private investigators, ones much less scrupulous than Anne Haynes. So yes, I helped him, even though I didn't much like what I found out. If you're going to blame anyone for this mess, blame Anne Haynes. It's her investigation that aroused Tim's curiosity, and that of countless others."

"What do you mean?"

"When I started to work on the story, I found out I wasn't the only one looking into it. A couple of rookies from the *Boston Globe* were blundering their way through an investigation, too. Don't worry. They didn't find anything, yet. But they'll hit the real story sooner or later and that's why I—I wrote it first."

"You what?" he thundered.

"It's going to be in the Monday morning edition of the Concord paper. There's every reason to believe it'll then be picked up by the Associated Press."

Along with her byline, John thought angrily, realizing how much oomph this would give Melinda's fledgling career. It was the big break she'd wanted. She'd get off the society column and back into politics. She'd certainly proven with this story she didn't spare anyone. Not even her ex-in-laws. "Does Tim know?" Fury gave his voice a hard edge.

"No, that's why I'm here. I thought you'd want to break it to him and to Gloria before it hits the papers."

"YOU KNEW about it, didn't you?" Tim said, once the news had sunk in. "You knew all along. That's why you didn't want me to search!"

At that moment, John hated Frank for his weakness in having an extramarital affair and for drawing him into this. Wishing with all his heart he could have spared his nephew this pain, John explained wearily, "I didn't want you to be hurt."

"No," Tim disagreed vehemently, advancing on him, dark eyes blazing, "you didn't want my sainted dad's memory to be hurt!" He balled both his hands into tight fists. "Damn him anyway, for lying to me!" he shouted.

"Tim—!"

"Get away from me!" Tim shouted. He struck out blindly, his fist contacting hard with John's jaw. "I don't want to hear anything you have to say!"

"Well, you're going to hear this," John countered. His jaw throbbed. He grabbed Tim's arms and pinned them to his sides to subdue the struggling teen. "Your father, God rest his soul, was no saint and he made a mistake, but he tried to do right by you in the end."

"The hell he did." Tim twisted away. Knowing Tim was beyond listening to reason at that point, John let him go.

Tim whirled, spitting his next words like shards of glass. "My father was nothing but a liar and a cheat! You hear me? Everything he stood for, everything he ever said he was, was a lie! A big, stupid lie! As far as I'm concerned, you're a liar, too!" Tim fled the room.

Knowing he couldn't begin to undo the damage his philandering older brother had done, John watched Tim go. Gloria appeared in the doorway. It was clear she had witnessed everything. Tears streamed down her face. "I agree with Tim," she sniffed, wiping her eyes. "Frank was a louse." She strangled a tissue in her hands. "How could he have done this to me?" she whispered hoarsely. "How could he have done this to us?"

John shook his head. "That's just it, Gloria, he didn't think. He—he went with the feelings he had at that moment, and at that moment, he was devastated by his inability to have a child. He was lonely, thousands of miles from his family, his wife and his friends." John knew it was no excuse, but it was the only one Frank had been able to give him.

"So he had a child with Son-ja! And then brought it home and passed it off as an orphan he'd become attached to while overseas? How gullible he must have thought me. How gullible I was! But you saw through him all along, didn't you?"

John sighed. Gloria was right. He had suspected something was up even before Frank had spilled his guts. The two of them had grown up together and he had been covering for Frank for a good many years. As for Gloria, it might have helped had Son-ja not been beautiful and cultured, but she was. And now that the two women had met, Gloria knew exactly who her competition for Frank's affections had been. It couldn't have been a good feeling. "I'm sorry, Gloria," he said sadly, wishing he could have spared her, too.

Gloria's face whitened furiously. "So am I."

John looked in the direction of the stairs and thought about his nephew. He'd been walking an emotional tightrope before. Now he seemed about to go over the edge completely. "About Tim—"

"I'll try to talk to him and calm him down," Gloria interrupted, "but I don't know if it's possible." She glared at John. "How could you have covered for him like that?" she demanded.

John knew how she felt. But he also knew she had to realize, deep down, that his first loyalty had to be to his brother. "I had no choice."

"Yes," she enunciated very clearly and very slowly, her eyes pinning him with her own, "you did."

Having no answer for that, he remained silent. He'd felt the best thing was to work to preserve Frank's marriage, and give Tim a loving home.

Gloria turned her back to him. "I think you'd better leave," she said stiffly. "Please, John, just go."

"I CAN'T SAY I blame her," Anne said an hour later when she'd heard everything. "Gloria has every right to be hurt. So does Tim."

John raked his hands through his hair, feeling very glad he had Anne to turn to. "I feel like such a louse."

She went to him and sat beside him on the sofa, covering his hand with her own. "You did what you thought was best, for Tim and your brother. Frank had to have someone to talk to."

John shook his head ruefully and held Anne's hand tightly. He found strength in just sitting next to her. "Maybe I should have convinced Frank to tell Gloria the truth."

Anne gave him a skeptical look. "And destroyed their marriage?" she whispered kindly. "I don't think so. You can't second-guess your actions. All you can do is accept it and move on."

He reached out to her. She moved into the circle of his arms, her body warm against the length of his, and pressed her cheek against his shirtfront. "I'm sorry your family is in so much pain," she murmured. She laced both her arms possessively around his middle.

John shut his eyes and held her even tighter, needing the warmth and comfort she could give. "We all have our crosses to bear, but this seems like a particularly painful one." He tangled his hands through the silk of her hair, letting its softness soothe his palms the way her comfort soothed his soul. He drew back, so she could see his eyes. "The worst of it is, I'm angry with Frank, too. I resent him for leaving me here to deal with this. I resent being stuck in the middle of his family problem."

She rested her palms on his upper arms, curving her fingers around his biceps. "I know they're angry with you, and they're saying a lot of hurtful things, but Tim and Gloria both need you. You've got to hang in there. They'll come around. You'll see."

John relaxed. "I don't know what I'd do if I couldn't talk to you," he whispered.

The phone rang. Reluctantly Anne went to get it. "Hello?" She listened a moment, then handed him the receiver. "For you. It's Gloria. She sounds upset."

John took the receiver, his eyes still on Anne's beautiful face. He listened intently, his mouth thinning. He had no choice but to go. "Sit tight. I'll be right there." He hung up to find Anne still watching him intently.

"What is it?" She knew from the distressed look on his face it was something very bad.

"It's Tim," John reported unhappily, not bothering to hide his disappointment and concern. "He's run away."

THE SITUATION at Gloria's home was every bit as chaotic as John feared. Now, he had not only Gloria to deal with but her three teenage daughters as well. Fortunately Anne had agreed to come with him, to lend a hand if need be.

"I don't see why you're so worried, Mom," Betsy was saying to her mother. Hope let John and Anne in the door. "You know he'll show up sooner or later."

Gloria whirled on her daughter, momentarily ignoring Anne and John. "Betsy, that's a terrible thing to say!" she accused, her face pale and strained.

"Well, it's true. I think Tim ought to be *happy* to find out that Dad was his real father," Betsy said. "And, anyway, isn't that what he's always wanted? To be one of us, biologically? Well, now he is!"

Fourteen-year-old Hope rolled her eyes. "Would you use your brain? Of course he's not happy. How could he be? The fact Tim is Dad's real son means *our sainted father—*" her voice dropped to a resentful whisper "*—fooled around while he was married!* And this, after all those lectures about how we Westfields should go out there and do some good! Well, he sure did some good, all right, didn't he?"

"Girls!" Looking tremendously upset, Gloria put her hands to her head, as if warding off a giant tension headache. "Please. Things are bad enough without you putting your two cents in."

John stepped beside his sister-in-law. "Your mother's right, girls. Why don't you all go upstairs and find something to do?"

The normally easygoing Susie glared at them. "Fine!" she said, seemingly hurt by being dismissed in the middle of a family crisis. "We will!"

John waited until the girls left. He turned back to Gloria. "They didn't mean to hurt you—"

"I know," Gloria said. She looked stronger than she had in weeks, as if the crisis and her concern for Tim had energized her and enabled her to really begin coping on her own again. "They're just trying to help. Unfortunately there's no way to do that, except to find Tim and bring him home." She shook her head ruefully. "How I wish I hadn't fallen apart earlier. Tim might not have run away. But I was so caught up in my own feelings..." Her voice trailed off wistfully. Sincere regret mingled with the pain in her face.

"You did the best you could," John said. He was very glad she had it together now.

"I know."

The rest of the night passed in a haze of black coffee and tense telephone calls. John told Anne she could go home, but she insisted on staying with them, and he was glad she did. Gloria was no longer blaming Anne. Now she blamed Frank. That made things easier, too. Near dawn, they received a call from a friend who owned a fishing lodge in Canada. He let them know Tim was there and could stay as long as he wanted.

"What now?" John asked, when Gloria had hung up. For the first time since his brother had died, he felt Gloria could cope.

"I'm going up there to be with him, of course."

There was a thud outside the front door as the newspaper landed. John went out to get it. He brought it in and unfolded it. He swore silently when he saw Melinda's article, with her byline, at the bottom of the front page.

John scanned the article, his elation over finding Tim fading fast. In all the excitement, he had almost forgotten they would have to deal with this today, as well.

Gloria scanned the article. "Thank heaven Tim isn't here to see this," she said quietly.

John glanced at his watch. It was still early. "If you hurry, you can get out of here before the other reporters descend."

Gloria nodded, already galvanized into action. "I want the girls out of here, too." She cast John a hesitant look. "I hate to ask. You've done so much already, but someone needs to take the girls up to the

Westfield compound, until the worst of this scandal passes."

"I'd be glad to do it," John said, feeling as though he could use some time alone, too. The security at the compound was such that no reporters would be able to trespass beyond the electric gates or high chain-link fence.

He turned to Anne, sorry he was going to have to be away from her, yet glad she was there to help him out with some of the details. "Do me a favor and tell Lily where I've gone. She'll know how to cancel all my appearances."

Anne nodded. "Sure."

John smiled and leaned forward to lightly kiss her cheek. *When this is all over*, he promised himself silently, *we will be together. One way or another, come hell or high water, I'll find a way to make it happen.*

"ANNE, I'm so glad to see you!" Lily said the moment Anne walked into the office Monday morning. Taking Anne's arm, she led her through the crowd of volunteers and reporters and pulled her into John's private office. "Did you see this morning's paper?"

"Unfortunately, yes," Anne said. She put her briefcase and purse down on the sofa. Knowing she'd had a part in the scandal, however incidental, made her feel terrible. And though Gloria had stopped blaming her, she couldn't stop blaming herself. It didn't matter that Tim would have gone to someone else. She had been a part of it, and now John's family was hurt. She had never wanted that to happen.

"I've been trying to get John all morning," Lily continued, wringing her hands. "But he's not home."

"I know. We were over at Gloria's." Lily looked at Anne sharply. Was that jealousy on her face? Anne wondered. Or simply concern for her boss and his family under these scandalous circumstances? "John sent you a message," Anne continued as calmly as possible. "He's taking his three nieces to the Westfield compound. He'll stay with them while they ride out the worst of the scandal."

Looking momentarily pacified, Lily asked softly, "What about Tim?"

"He's in Canada. His mother went there to be with him."

"Oh." She took a moment to sort it all out, then turned to Anne, still looking a little bewildered and upset. "Why didn't John call me himself?"

Anne saw Lily was hurt. Maybe she had a reason to be. After all, before Anne and John had started getting close, John had confided all his family problems in Lily. Anne had never meant to edge Lily out, but now there was really no need for John to confide in Lily, not as regularly and intimately as he had before. "He was in a hurry to get the girls out of there," she explained kindly. "With them all packing at once, it was a little chaotic and crazy." Especially since the three teenage girls did not want to go to Lake Winnipesaukee.

"Oh," Lily said.

Wanting to comfort her, Anne found herself saying, "I'm sure John will check in with you later today, when things calm down."

Lily heartened and pulled herself together. "You're probably right," she said more cheerfully. She riffled through the telephone messages she had in her hand. "Did he know how long he'd be gone?"

Anne shrugged. She was going to miss John more than Lily. Much more. It was so frustrating to feel them getting closer and closer, only to have their lives disrupted. But maybe that was normal, too, at least for a man in the midst of a campaign for governor. Anne finally said, "He wasn't sure how long he'd be gone. Maybe a couple of days." And she would be counting every minute.

"I HATE BEING STUCK out here in the middle of nowhere!" sixteen-year-old Susie cried.

"You love it here," John countered incredulously. He couldn't remember a time when all three of the girls hadn't had a fabulous time out there. Of course he couldn't ever remember them being so difficult, moody and temperamental, either.

"Sure, when there are tons of people here and we're having one of our family parties! Not when we're stranded out here alone!"

"Yeah," Betsy added, aimlessly kicking a soccer ball around the cavernous living room. "There aren't even enough people here to play a decent game."

"Maybe we should watch a movie," John said, going to the videotape cabinet.

Fourteen-year-old Hope shook her head. "I'm not in the mood," she announced petulantly.

"Neither am I," Susie added.

"Well, what are you in the mood for?" John asked, exasperated. It was hard to cope when everyone around him was acting so depressed.

"I don't know. I'm going to take a shower," Susie stormed.

"Yeah," Betsy mumbled under her breath, still kicking the soccer ball around the living room. "Maybe she'll feel better if she washes her hair." She finished her sentence in a la-dee-dah tone.

Susie whirled. "I heard that, you little brat."

"Girls, girls." John stepped between them and held up his hands, stop-sign fashion.

"They can't help it, they're both dorks," Hope muttered in disgust. She stomped off in the direction of the library. "I'm going to try to find something to read!"

"You'd think Mom would've realized we'd have nothing to do up here with you," Betsy mumbled under her breath, stomping off after Hope.

John silently concurred. Why in blazes had he supposed he could do this? He had never tried to play mother to anyone before, never mind three teenage girls in the midst of an emotional crisis. What they needed was their mother. He was a poor substitute and they all knew it.

He sat down with paper and pen to think about solutions. Hopefully, if he just got organized, he'd come up with a solid, workable approach for managing the girls. Unfortunately his planning session accomplished nil. Moments later, the girls were all back, competing for his attention and sympathy as loudly as ever. "There aren't any Doritos to eat!" Betsy complained. "If I'm going to be stuck out here, I need Oreos, spreadable cheese and root beer!"

John grimaced at the combination, but he dutifully wrote down the asked-for items, reminding himself that after the shock the girls had suffered they had a right to be surly and ill-tempered. At least, unlike Tim, they weren't asking him to explain Frank's actions.

"As long as you're going to the store, I need shampoo, conditioner and a bunch of other stuff," Susie said. She thrust an incredibly long list at him.

"And I want some decent romance novels to read," Hope added. "I'm not reading that Mark Twain blather that's in the library."

"*Huck Finn*'s a classic!"

Hope rolled her eyes as if that said it all in her estimation. "Exactly."

Sighing, John got his car keys and headed off to the store. None of the girls wanted to go with him, which was just as well. They weren't the best of company and after being around them most of the night and half the day, neither was he. Once at the store, however, his predicament only got worse.

He couldn't find any of the authors Hope had written on her list, so he had to try to pick and choose among the teen romance titles. It wasn't an easy task for someone who much preferred sci-fi and adventure novels. Sure Hope would hate all six of the books he

Home Free

had picked out, he moved on to the snack aisle, where he dutifully picked up Doritos, spreadable cheese and Oreos. He added potato chips and dip for himself. Wheeling over to the beverage aisle, he loaded up on carbonated drinks. His cart was getting pretty full and he still had to get the things Susie wanted. Pulling her list from his pocket, he went over to the cosmetics aisle. The shampoo and conditioner were easy. The nail polish and lipstick a little harder, but it was the last article on the list, the request for maxi-pads, that was the real killer.

I can do this, John told himself firmly, trying hard not to turn red with embarrassment. I'll just go over to the feminine products aisle, grab a box and get the hell out of there.

Only it wasn't that simple, he soon found out. There were dozens and dozens of kinds of maxi-pads. He hadn't a clue as to what kind.

"You look a little lost. May I help you?" an efficient-looking female clerk not much older than his nieces said at his elbow.

Despite his effort to play it cool, John felt himself turn redder. Somehow he managed to spit out the words, but he couldn't bring himself to make eye contact with the clerk, who was staring at him curiously. "I need to get some maxi-pads for my niece."

"Some what?" She leaned closer and peered at him closely.

Unwilling to go through this any more than necessary, John took a deep breath and spoke a little louder. "Some maxi-pads."

"Oh!" Fighting to stifle a sympathetic laugh, the clerk turned away from him. "I see your dilemma. Do you know what brand?" Her attitude was officious when she turned back to him.

Feeling more embarrassed and out of his element than he ever had in his entire life, John stared at the shelves. "She didn't specify," he answered quietly. And idiot that he was, he hadn't thought to ask. Of course he hadn't known diddly about the sheer number of selections.

"I see." The young clerk cast a wondering look at the amount of junk food and sundry items, especially the teen romances, in his cart, then turned back to the shelves. She started handing him boxes. "Well, there are the kind with the thin adhesive strips," she explained, keeping her back to him. She looked about as comfortable making the explanation as he was getting it. "Thick or thin pads, of course." She handed him a pink box, then an aqua one. "We have the super absorbent fibers, and the deodorant and nondeodorant pads." She handed him various boxes. "And, of course, the quilted type. Some ladies really like them. Just kind of depends." The clerk shrugged, waiting for him to make an informed decision.

I am in my worst nightmare, John thought. There was no way he wanted to read the backs of those boxes or think about all those options, or what the consequences might be if he showed up at the compound with the wrong type. Susie really would come unglued, and it would be all his fault. For the first time, he had total sympathy for Gloria.

Home Free 181

"I'll just take one of each," he decided hastily. He piled them all into his cart, wanting to get out of there before he was subjected to any more explanations, or worse, ran into someone he knew.

The clerk looked at him dubiously, no doubt thinking him even weirder for taking them all. "Well, if you're sure."

He was. He wanted the hell out of there. Unfortunately when he got home he was not exactly received with open arms. The girls frowned in dismay as they inspected the purchases. "You got the wrong kinds of pads!" Susie stormed, not caring a whit about the trauma she'd put him through. "I hate those. And the lipstick is all wrong! I said pink, not carnation! Plain pink!" With tears in her eyes, she stomped off.

"Didn't they have any better romance novels than these?" Hope complained. "Who cares about the problems of teen fashion models in the South Pacific or a dork without a boyfriend on prom night! I wanted to read about girl athletes who have boy problems!" She, too, burst into tears.

John glanced at Betsy. She was studying the root beer and Doritos he'd bought with a downcast expression. "What?" he prodded, knowing from the look on her face there was something wrong.

"I hate the salsa flavored chips—they're too spicy, and that root beer has an aftertaste like formaldehyde." She shrugged her shoulders dispiritedly, adding with a loud, tearful sniff, "But I know you did your best." Head bowed in abject misery, she went off to join her sisters.

John sat down at the table and buried his head in his hands. Three days. He had promised Gloria he would do this for three whole days. How in hell was he going to last?

"YOU'RE LEAVING, just like that?" Lily asked incredulously as Anne packed up her briefcase.

Anne had missed John terribly in the past thirty-six hours. Hearing from him had been a balm to her heart and soul. Knowing he wanted her with him—now, tonight—had been even more thrilling and exciting. Not wanting to make too much of his request, Anne worked to contain the elation in her voice. "John needs me to help him manage the girls in Gloria's absence," she explained. "And once things are a little calmer, we can work on his speeches for next week. He'll write them and I'll type them for him. With you here to run the office and keep the reporters at bay, we should be fine."

Lily nodded, looking unhappy but accepting the arrangement John wanted. "Well," she said at last, "tell John if he needs me there, I'll come up, too."

"I will," Anne promised, anxious to get out of the office and on her way to John. She'd never known there could be such pleasure in simply being needed. Maybe that was because she had never been needed in quite this way before.

"And Anne?" Lily said, breaking into Anne's thoughts.

Anne turned. "Yes?"

Lily hesitated and bit her lip. Finally she said, "Take care of him, okay?"

Anne nodded, knowing how much Lily and everyone else there at campaign headquarters cared about him. She'd do her best.

Chapter Ten

"Why are you girls giving your uncle John such a hard time?" Anne asked after John had finished filling her in. She'd gathered them in one of the upstairs bedrooms for a little woman-to-woman talk. She searched each of their faces in turn. "You know he's doing his best to take care of you."

Despite her attempt to make eye contact with the girls, none of them would look at her. In this case, she thought, that was a good sign. It meant they were already coming to their senses. "Susie, did you really expect him to be able to pick out lipstick or maxi-pads?" Anne questioned gently.

Susie blushed and squirmed a little at the idea of John floundering in the maxi-pads aisle of the grocery. "Well, no, I guess not," she admitted sheepishly, her cheeks pink with embarrassment.

"And what about you, Hope? You know he doesn't know anything about teen romance novels. Couldn't you have just said thank you?"

"Yeah, I guess."

"Betsy?"

"You're right," Betsy said. She stared steadfastly at the toes of her sneakers. "I should have told him what kind of Doritos to get and what brand of root beer. I knew there were different kinds."

"And barring that, thanked him for whatever he brought home." Anne faced the girls. She had been around them enough to know that they were nosy and lively and rambunctious to a fault, but they were also basically well mannered and well intentioned. They knew when they were being impossible and when they weren't. Judging from the guilty looks on their faces, all three had given John a hard time deliberately. "Don't you think you should be doing your best to make this situation a little easier?" she continued gently, "instead of harder on everyone concerned?"

"It's not our fault our mom went off and left us," Susie blurted out.

"Yeah," Betsy chimed in, "she should be here taking care of us."

"Instead of only Tim," Hope added resentfully. "I mean, we're her kids, too, and she just ran off and left us."

"So you're feeling left out and abandoned?"

Miserably, the girls nodded. "I guess we were acting like brats," Susie said.

"It really wasn't fair of us," Betsy added, ashamed.

"Well, it's nothing an apology and a good attitude from here on out won't fix," Anne said. "What do you say we go downstairs and make dinner a joint effort tonight? Okay? Who knows, maybe your mom will call later.''

As it happened, Gloria did call. The girls talked to her one by one, and after they'd hung up, they all felt a lot better, so much so that they went upstairs without a complaint to listen to records.

After the dishes were done, John led Anne to the covered back porch. It stretched the length of the imposing old house. He settled her beside him in a hanging swing.

"This morning I never would've believed I'd get through this day," he said. The twilight descended around them and the two of them swung back and forth and looked contentedly out at the lake. He snaked his arm across the back of the wooden seat, drawing her in closer to his side. "What'd you say to them, anyway?"

Anne grinned. "I just told them to cut you some slack."

He laughed, amused. "Did you now?"

"Yes. They were really mean to you today, weren't they?"

He shook his head ruefully, reflecting, "I admit I've never felt so out of place in my life. The worst moment was in the feminine products aisle of the grocery. I was as red as a beet, I think."

"Couldn't fit in, hmm?"

"No. And I'll tell you, I learned something from that. Before now, I felt all you had to do was *act* at ease and you would *be* at ease. I thought you could make yourself fit in somewhere just by *wanting* to fit in. No more. I'd never manage to be cool and collected in that aisle, no matter how long I live. That just isn't the place for me!"

Anne laughed softly, amused by his antics and aware there was a message beneath his words. "I'm sorry they put you through that," she said, turning to better see his face in the dimming light.

He stroked his hand down the side of her face, gently tracing her profile. "I'm not," he confessed, his eyes scanning her face reverently, lingering on her mouth before returning to her eyes. "Those antics of theirs got you up here with me."

He leaned closer, brushing her mouth with his own. "And that's exactly where I want you, Anne. Up here." He kissed her again, more soundly this time. "With me. In my arms."

It was where she wanted to be, too, and as he continued to kiss her, she felt herself soften from head to toe. She scooted even closer to him on the swing. She'd necked before, but never like this. She'd never allowed herself to go past that invisible line and let herself become completely vulnerable to anyone. She'd never risked her heart. And yet as his mouth moved over hers, softly at first, tenderly, then with increasing ardor, she felt it was okay to do just that. Suddenly she wasn't afraid to risk, let herself go and give in to the moment. She wasn't afraid of him or how she might react if he ever left. No matter what happened in the future, she would never regret this moment with him. Never.

Able to feel the change in her, John drew back. He looked down at her and his eyes became hot, possessive. His hands left her shoulders and stroked the length of her sides all the way down to her waist. His fingertips grazed only the outer curves of her breasts, but it was enough to set her on fire. Desire swept through her, and she felt her heart skip a beat.

He gave her a crooked grin. "Damn, but I wish we weren't the baby-sitters," he murmured.

She nodded her head, whispering back, "I know exactly what you mean." But even that didn't stop her from twining her arms around his neck. I just want one more kiss, she thought. One to hold me until we're alone again, just the two of us.

He took her mouth again and the kiss turned hard, as relentless and all-encompassing as the desire inundating them both. Weakness stole through her, centering in her knees, making even the thought of flight impossible. There was a fluttery, vacant feeling in the pit of her stomach. And a hunger deep inside her that just wouldn't be slaked.

She hadn't come to the lake intending for anything to happen. She'd expected to lend a hand with the girls. She'd expected to get closer to him, but she hadn't expected to sit in the porch swing with him and feel this incredible pleasure, this lightning bolt of need and yearning. She hadn't expected him to give of himself so completely or for her to do the same.

And yet reality intruded on them just the same. The sound of the stereo upstairs echoed throughout the still night. Voices followed. The thought of the example they'd be setting for the three impressionable teens finally drove her from his arms.

Having come to his senses, too, John drew back slowly, his breathing as ragged as her own. "Now I'm wishing we weren't here," he said huskily.

Her own body throbbing with need, Anne let out a shaky sigh. "I'm wishing that, too." She wanted to be with him, as close as two people could be. She was falling in love with John. Wise or not, that was just the way it was.

THE NEXT THREE DAYS passed blissfully enough, with Lily sending work out for John by daily courier. Anne and John alternately worked together and spent time with the girls. They had some cutthroat games of tennis, volleyball, backgammon and chess, split the cooking and cleanup duties and generally got along with one another. Evenings were theirs alone, though, and they generally spent them alternately talking and necking on the porch swing. Anne had never been so emotionally content in her life, or so sexually frustrated, and it was with mixed feelings that she greeted Gloria late Friday morning. She wanted to leave their little acre of paradise, and she didn't.

"Where's Tim?" John asked Gloria as she helped herself to a cup of coffee in the kitchen. The girls, who'd been up late the evening before, watching a Tom Cruise double feature on cable, were still sleeping soundly even though it was nearly noon. Anne and John had both been up, dressed and working on campaign business for hours.

"He's decided to spend the rest of the summer working at the fishing lodge in Canada. To tell you the truth, he's not sure he wants to come back." She ended on a note of ragged pain.

"I'm sorry," Anne said softly. She had never meant for any of this to happen. She wasn't to blame—they all knew Tim would have found out the truth one way or another eventually—but she felt bad about the situation, anyway. So did John.

Gloria no longer blamed Anne for her son's problems. "Thanks," she said quietly. Looking down into her coffee, she gave a helpless little shrug. "I wish he had come back with me. Lord knows I tried to get him to, but he said he needed time. I guess after all that's happened, I can't blame him."

"He'll come around," John comforted.

"Maybe." Gloria frowned. "But the truth is I need time, too. Frank's betrayal is very hard for me to deal with." Without warning, her eyes filled with tears. "I always thought we had such a good marriage, that it was rock solid. I guess I was wrong."

Anne searched for a way to console her. "You were both awfully young at the time—"

"That's no excuse." Gloria shook her head, taking a deep draught of her coffee. "It doesn't matter how young we were or whether it was one infidelity or ten. Frank still betrayed our marriage vows. And you, John," she leveled him a censuring look, "knew about it and helped cover for him." Not giving him a chance to respond, she put her cup into the sink, pivoted and headed for the door. "I'm going to check on the girls."

John stalked out onto the porch. Anne followed him. "She'll get over this," she said firmly.

John turned to face her. He rested a hand on either side of the porch railing behind him. His fingers curled tightly around the painted wood. "Right now I want to strangle my brother for putting us all through this," he said grimly.

Anne shared that feeling, although she knew her emotion wasn't nearly as strong as his own. "We can't undo the past, no matter how much we want to." How well she knew that.

John held open his arms in silent entreaty and she moved into them. He pulled her close, his breath warm on her hair. "Have I told you today how glad I am you're here with me?" he asked softly.

"Yes," Anne smiled, lifting her face for the kiss she knew was coming. She twined her arms around his neck and let out a contented breath. "But you can tell me again and again and again." She would never tire of hearing it.

"AND THEN you've got the dinner at the American Legion hall at nine," Lily said Saturday morning as she finished catching John up-to-date on his revamped schedule.

"Okay. Tell them I'll be bringing a date," John said.

Lily was too polite to ask, but John could see the question in her eyes. "Anne and I have become a steady thing," he said. "From now on, you'll need to schedule her in on all my evening activities."

"I see." Lily held her back stiffly and got up and went over to her desk.

John could tell she disapproved. It wasn't her place to do so, but he wanted whatever she was feeling out in the open. "If something's on your mind," he prodded gruffly, "say it."

Lily turned. "I'm not sure I should." She paused and straightened the papers in her hand. "You're entitled to a personal life, even in the midst of a campaign."

The phone rang. Looking relieved at the diversion, Lily picked it up and was soon immersed in more business.

John waited patiently for his assistant to get off the phone. Far from angry with her, he thought he knew what she was trying to tell him. It was a risk to become involved with anyone at this particular stage of the game. In the months left before the election, he would be campaigning nonstop all over the state. The press would be with him night and day. If they thought he was serious about Anne—and after their time at the lake together, he privately acknowledged that he was— they would be scrutinizing her background, too.

That kind of attention from the press was hard for anyone to take. It would be doubly so for Anne, who had never been truly comfortable in the limelight. And yet, he had the feeling that given time she could learn to cope with the demands of public life. Certainly, it wouldn't be easy for her. But unlike Melinda, who had resented his career and his family from day one, Anne was already becoming involved. She cared about his nieces and Tim. She'd even made her peace with Gloria. And she had a lot of love locked up inside her, love that unless he missed his guess, she was just aching to give. He knew how important her work with Amerasians was. He would never ask her to give that up. He might even be able to help her fund it....

Just as Lily got off the phone, Anne walked in. She beamed as she looked at him. He couldn't help but notice she had an envelope clasped tightly in her hand. Sensing the two of them wanted to be alone, Lily excused herself and shut the door. "You'll never guess what happened today!" Anne announced happily.

"Probably not," John agreed drolly.

Anne thrust the envelope at him. "Take a look," she instructed buoyantly. Curious, he opened it. Inside was a check for ten thousand dollars, from Robert Ryan.

"It's for my foundation!"

John shared her euphoria. "Did you get a letter with it or anything?" He knew how hurt she'd been when her father rejected her. Obviously now that he'd had time to think about it, Robert Ryan had realized how wrong he had been to dismiss her so abruptly.

Anne shook her head. "No, but—the money—John, it has to be a sign that he's coming around, that he believes in what I'm doing."

"I'm happy for you, Annie." John held out his arms. Anne went into them gladly.

"Now I won't have to take any outside work for quite a while," Anne continued. After the hardship of working two jobs, it would be heaven to concentrate only on her cases again and devote herself entirely to helping other Amerasians.

"Does this mean—?" John paused, his expression grim.

"I won't quit until after the Fourth," Anne promised. As much as she wanted to get back to Answers, Inc., she'd made a commitment to John and she would honor it.

"Thank goodness for that." John breathed a sigh of relief, then took another closer look at her face. "What about Robert Ryan? Have you called him?"

Anne's smile faded, but she kept up the cheerful facade. "I tried. He's out of town."

"Are you disappointed he didn't give you the check personally?" John asked.

She nodded, refusing to let herself be discouraged. The look in her dark blue eyes was distant. "But maybe under the circumstances this is best, for now," she said quietly.

Maybe it was and maybe it wasn't. John had the feeling Anne and her natural father still had a lot to deal with, and that their mutual anxiety wouldn't fade until they talked. Still, he wasn't about to spoil her joy about the contribution. "About tonight," John continued casually, "I've got a dinner at the American Legion hall. I'm supposed to make a speech and I want you to go with me as my date."

Her eyes held his. She realized without being told what a commitment this was on his part. He'd be announcing to the world that he was serious about her. Was she ready for that? Were they?

Aware her heart was pounding furiously, Anne took a deep breath, fighting her fear that she wouldn't be good enough, that she'd somehow make a mistake. She loved John. She could do this. She only had to try. "I'd like that very much. But right now, I've got a lot of work to do."

"Me, too." He reached forward and caught her hand. Reeling her in to his side, he gave her a quick kiss on the brow. "See you later?"

Anne smiled, not letting go of his hand until the very last minute. "You can bet on it."

Unfortunately the afternoon brought a host of work-related problems. A new poll came out, showing John had dropped five points in the polls as a result of the recent scandal involving his brother. It wasn't a trend that couldn't be remedied, but it had everyone a little depressed just the same. Also, John's stand on continued equal pay and equal rights for women and state-subsidized child-care facilities had brought him a lot of flak from his opponent. His opponent was launching an attack that bordered on ludicrous. "Did you read this?" one of John's staffers said, outraged, holding up the latest newspaper interview. "The jerk says John is trying to destroy the American family by encouraging women to enter the work force."

Lily sighed and rolled her eyes, looking every bit the experienced staffer she was. "I wonder what they'd like him to say," she commented dryly.

"Probably something like women belong in the kitchen, barefoot and pregnant," joked a staffer.

There was a round of laughter. "No, no, I have it," another staffer said, rolling a sheet of paper into the typewriter. Speaking in a parody of a television reporter, the staffer composed off the top of his head as he typed, "John Westfield, noted politician, announced today he has renounced his previous stand on the American family. He believes it shouldn't exist—"

Anne rolled her eyes, as did everyone else in the room. She tried, with little success, to go back to the list of organized activities she was setting up for the Fourth.

"Except," added another staffer, laughing, "where women exist only to serve their man—"

"And have babies—"

"And scrub floors—"

"After all," continued the staffer who was still typing, "we all know women can't possibly be as smart or as capable as men—"

This got a groan from all. Several women picked up wadded scraps of paper and hurled them at the men. Lily laughed and joked along with them for several minutes, but eventually retrieved the bogus press release. She cheerfully ordered them all back to work. When all was calm again, Lily retreated into John's office to show him the release, so he'd get a laugh, too.

Home Free

That evening, Anne put on her prettiest outfit, a pale yellow linen sleeveless dress with a matching jacket. Striving for a more elegant look, she twisted her dark hair into a loose topknot, then tugged tiny strands free, to curl around her face and at the nape. Chunky gold earrings and a matching necklace completed her ensemble. John whistled when he came to pick her up. Added color flowed into her cheeks.

"You look terrific," he said, kissing her wrist.

"So do you," Anne said softly.

The evening was blissful. The group at the American Legion Hall was comprised entirely of John's supporters, so both he and his speech were received enthusiastically.

"Can you believe it?" John said later, when they'd returned to her place for a nightcap. "Not only are they not fighting it, but they gave money for the low-income housing project."

"It was no surprise to me," Anne said, sliding her finger around the rim of a brandy glass. "You're a very eloquent speaker."

He smiled in a sad sort of way. He was clearly worried about his recent drop in the polls. "You think so?"

"Yes," Anne said softly. She'd never seen him more vulnerable than at that moment. It amazed her that with all his confidence he could worry about anything. "I do." She looked into his face and saw his eyes soften in relief and gratitude. Like her, he sometimes just needed to hear the words. He just needed to know that someone believed in him, through thick or thin. And she did believe in John so much.

He shifted closer, his mouth slanting over hers. At first taste, she knew kissing would not be enough. She wanted him, body and soul. And for the first time, there was no reason to stop. She knew she wanted to make love with him. She knew it would be perfect. And the joy and rightness of being with him flowed through her, chasing away the last of her butterflies, relaxing her like fine wine.

When he finally raised his head to look at her again, nothing was suppressed. Though neither had yet said the words, she thought she knew what it meant to love and be loved. She liked the feeling very much. She yearned for more. As he helped her out of her jacket, his lips touched the curve of her shoulder. "Your skin is like silk." And his kiss, Anne thought, was like fire.

"Do these hurt?" he whispered curiously, touching the clasp on her chunky gold earring. She knew he had noticed her fiddling with them all evening, but it wasn't so much that the clasps were too tight. Her nervousness and the building lasciviousness of her thoughts had kept her reaching for them again and again.

Mesmerized by the intensity of his gaze, she was aware she didn't want to take them off so much as she wanted him to take them off. "A little."

He smiled and promised, "I'll make it better." He took off her earrings and kissed each lobe in turn. She let her head fall back. The worries she'd felt earlier about not being right for him faded. She would think about those things later and figure a way to work everything out. Tonight was for love.

Moving behind her, he kissed the back of her neck until it tingled, too. He trailed his lips back and forth over the tender, exposed skin. "What about this?" he asked, both hands circling the chunky gold necklace, tracing it from her nape to the sloping vee of her breasts.

Anne closed her eyes, reveling in the luxurious feeling of his hands resting on the upper curves of her breasts. His body behind hers, so close that she felt sensations of warmth, strength and hard masculinity. She sighed. "It can go, too."

Her breasts and thighs ached for more as he managed the simple clasp and put it aside. His patience fading at long last, he turned her to face him. She glanced up at him, her head tipped back in unconscious invitation. He whispered her name, once, and then his mouth was on hers, hot and wet and urgent. "I knew it would be like this," he murmured, as her insides turned to liquid.

Anne sighed. "Then you were one up on me." She still didn't know quite what to expect, only that she wanted to find out... and soon. As his arms wrapped around her, she moaned her acquiescence. She felt robbed of all will except for the primal, untutored need that welled within her. She needed him, more than life. And so, it seemed, as the kiss went on and on, did he.

He reached up and released the pins that held her hair. The dark, silky mass fell around her shoulders.

He arranged the strands with a deft artist's touch, taking his time, until at last he was satisfied. Finished, he looked at her in quiet adoration. She felt more beautiful than she ever had in her life and was filled with gratitude to him for giving her that.

He drew her to him and kissed her again, lingeringly this time. Her lips clung to his. She wrapped her arms around his neck, knowing it was time, past time, and that there was no one else for her, nor had there ever been. And John seemed to know it, too.

Wordlessly he scooped her in his arms and carried her upstairs to her bedroom. She was shy. He let her leave the light off, so the room was lit only by the moonlight shimmering in through the drapes.

Disrobing was easy. Touching, easier still. His hands stroked her body. Her hands stroked his, exploring, learning. He felt silky hard and hot against the cradle of her thighs. She wondered if it would hurt and knew she didn't really care, so long as she was with him. It was time she learned about love.

JOHN LAY WITH ANNE curled against his side, her head on his chest. The tears on her face were still salty and damp and he knew without looking that the sheet beneath them was damp, too. He wished he'd known. But he didn't, not when she'd sobbed her pleasure as she climaxed, or later, when she urged him inside her. And now that the barrier had been breached, there was no going back. Her life had changed forever. "Why didn't you tell me?" he asked quietly, silently damning himself for not having known. How could he not have realized she was as virgin as new-fallen snow?

As always, when they came to a subject she didn't want to discuss, Anne moved as if to run away. She rolled away from him and clutched the sheet to her breast. She sat on the edge of the bed with her back to him. She looked out into the moonlight, letting the curtain of dark silky hair hide her face. "There was nothing to tell," she denied quietly.

Like hell there wasn't, John thought. Sensing she was about to put even more distance between them, he caught her wrist and held her there. He knew he'd hurt her, getting past the barrier of her virginity, but he wouldn't ever hurt her again, not in that way. "Annie," he urged softly. He stroked the naked silk of her arm, from her shoulder to her back. "Talk to me, sweetheart. Please. Tell me. Why now?"

She turned. The wonder she'd felt earlier shone briefly in her eyes. He thought for a moment she was going to tell him she loved him, that she would give him what no woman ever had and sacrifice everything and anything to be with him. But she didn't. And it was all he could do to hide his disappointment.

"Why not?" she retorted softly with a playfulness meant to cover her uneasiness. She brought a foot up on the bed and rested her chin on her bent knee. "Don't you think it was about time?"

Yes, John thought, it was about time they expressed their growing commitment to each other and made love. But that wasn't what they were talking about and she knew it. They were talking about all the years that had come before and all the men she'd undoubtedly turned down.

"Why not sooner?" he asked when she still didn't answer. After all, she was a grown woman. But had waited until now. As awed and honored as that made him feel, it also made him feel responsible for her continued happiness and well-being. And he wouldn't be able to follow through unless he understood her reasons. His gut instincts were telling him that this decision of hers was all wrapped up in how she felt about herself.

"I didn't want to be like my mother," she said quietly, her head bent. He waited, knowing without her telling him that there was more. She wet her lips and continued with effort, "I didn't want my being with someone to be insignificant. I wanted it to mean something...to be with someone special...and so I waited." Her soft, simple tone laced its way around his heart and made her his forever, "I waited for the right time, the right place and you."

John's heart soared at the realization of how much she cared about him, but what she felt about herself and her origins troubled him deeply. "What makes you think your mother's relationship with your father was insignificant?" John wished he had a magic way to make her feel good about every aspect of her past.

"If it hadn't been, he would've rejoiced at having found me," she whispered.

Home Free   203

Back to her dream, John thought, the one she'd had since her mother had died and still couldn't quite give up. She wanted to be close to her natural father. He wanted that for her, the same way he wanted her to have anything she wanted. He was disappointed it wasn't happening sooner, but he also knew there was reason now to hope. "Robert Ryan gave you a donation," John reminded patiently.

"I know." Anne's disappointment faded as quickly as it had appeared and her look gentled. She turned and climbed back into bed with him. Her body was chilled. She aligned herself with him and took of his warmth. "I thought at first it was a sign he was coming around, too," she said, her teeth chattering slightly. "But then the more I thought about it, the more I realized it could just be hush money, to ensure I wouldn't talk. Who knows? Maybe he's trying to assuage his conscience for all the years of neglect. Maybe I was just fooling myself, thinking the donation was a sign of his acceptance."

John fell silent. He knew what it had cost Anne to be candid with him about that. He was glad she trusted him enough to confide in him. He wished he could erase the past, but all he could control was the future. Wrapping both arms around her, he rolled her toward him and held her tightly. "I'm glad I was the first, Annie," he whispered, pressing a kiss into her hair. And he would make it better for her the next time. The next time she would have pleasure before, during and after their bodies merged, not just before.

And there would be a next time, he promised himself silently. Just as soon as she had healed.

She looked up at him, touching her hand to the side of his face. All the love she felt in her heart was expressed in her dark midnight-blue eyes. "I'm glad you were the first, too, John," she whispered, the words coming from her soul. "Very, very glad."

UFORTUNATELY, the office was a zoo when they got in Monday morning. Lily was in a phenomenally bad mood. Two thousand envelopes had been mailed out to registered voters without the enclosed letter. A second mailing had to begin at once. Everyone was typing furiously on their own stack of letters. Anne, realizing the urgency of righting the mistake, volunteered to put her own work aside and help with the repeat mass mailing. But Lily, already overworked and determined to supervise the mass mailing herself, had something far more important for Anne to do.

"I need someone I can trust on this," Lily said, handing Anne the press releases she and John had composed the previous day. The releases defended John's stand on subsidized child care and women's rights. "They've already been printed," Lily said. "All you have to do is go down the list, type up one envelope for every name on the list and enclose the release, seal and stamp. You'll have to work fast because we want the first batch at the post office by noon." She tossed a finished envelope on Anne's desk, then started a second and third.

Home Free

Marveling at the quickness with which Lily was able to get out the releases, Anne began. She made her deadline, but barely, then stayed around the rest of the afternoon to help Lily and the rest of the staff finish their mailing.

"You're due over at the Heights this evening to give them a hand assembling the wooden playground equipment that was donated," Lily reminded John as the office volunteers and paid campaign workers began to leave.

"Thanks, Lil." John turned to Anne. "Want to go with me?"

The look in his eyes reminded her of the intimacy they had shared over the weekend. They'd been together Saturday night and all of Sunday, too.

Aware Lily and a few others were watching them surreptitiously, Anne forced herself to focus on John's question. "I'm not very handy with a hammer." She wanted to go. She just didn't want to embarrass him or make it obvious, in public, that the two of them had begun an affair.

"No problem," John reassured her pleasantly. "They'll take beginners, too." He turned to his assistant. "What about you, Lily? Want to go?"

"No, I'll pass," Lily said, turning away. "I still have a lot of work to do."

Able to see Lily was still upset about the screwup with the last mailing, John and Anne said nothing more. Finished with their own work, they went home to change and grab a quick bite to eat. They arrived at the Heights a little after six-thirty.

"The place looks so much nicer," Anne murmured. She had known people were working on it, but she hadn't been out to see it.

"Amazing what a new coat of paint and a little soap and water will do, isn't it?" John murmured. He was glad his continued work had inspired the current residents to take a little more pride in their environment.

As for the playground, that, too, was coming along splendidly. A large wooden fort was already up and a matching wooden swing set was currently being assembled. At the other end of the newly enclosed playground, residents and some volunteers from Unified Electronics were working on a structure that resembled a ship. Anne and John's help was accepted readily and for the next two hours they hammered, carried and sanded right along with everyone else. Around dark, they called it quits for the day.

Once back at her house, Anne wanted to invite John in, but again the never-ending demands of his campaign interfered. He had a meeting with Lily and his advisers to plan his next series of television commercials, and just enough time to make it back to his place, shower and change. "I'll see you in the morning," he promised, giving her a quick kiss.

Anne spent a quiet night alone, drafting more letters for Trong. Her mood was still wistful and subdued when she got to campaign headquarters the following morning. She wasn't making nearly the progress on Trong's case she wanted, and it didn't help that John had a breakfast meeting and would be coming in late. Determined not to let his life-style bother her, she busied herself arranging for a stage to be built for the musicians entertaining on the Fourth. She had just finished when John came in. He stopped by her desk. "Hi."

"Hi."

He smiled. *There's so much I wish I could say right now.*

I know.

I love you.

I love you, too.

"John?" Lily was at his side, sounding a little harried. "There's a reporter here to see you."

John turned. His expression grew serious. He focused on his assistant. "Did I have an interview scheduled?"

"No, but he says it's urgent."

John looked puzzled. "Okay. Tell him I'll be right in."

"That isn't necessary," a well-dressed man said, coming out of John's office. Anne recognized him immediately as a columnist for the Manchester paper, one of the largest in the state. "In fact, if it's okay with you, I'd prefer to have this interview right here. It concerns one of the vital issues of your campaign." Reaching into his pocket, he withdrew an envelope bearing John's name. "I'd like to talk to you about your remarks in your latest press release. It's the one I received in this morning's mail. It was postmarked yesterday."

Which meant, Anne thought, that she had to have been the one who typed it and sent it out. She'd sent out all the latest press releases. Oh, no, she thought, with a sinking feeling of dread, what have I done?

Ron Simon was already continuing, reading from the release he held in his hand. "It says, and I quote, 'We all know women aren't as smart as men.' Could you elaborate on that?"

John stared at him. "What are you talking about?"

"That's what I'd like to know." Ron Simon handed the paper to John, for his perusal. The color left John's face as he glanced at the press release. He recognized it as the office prank that had been hilariously typed—and supposedly destroyed—the previous week.

Anne realized that the prank release had gotten mixed up with real campaign papers. She knew how devastated John felt. Oh God, why had she been in such a hurry? Why hadn't she checked every single release before folding it and placing it in the envelope, instead of just assuming they were all the same? The misery she felt made her ill.

Lily was as white as a sheet, too. "This is all a big mistake," Lily protested. "A joke!"

"Then these remarks are not a reflection of your campaign policy?" Ron Simon ascertained, retrieving the letter.

"Of course not," John said. "I would never say anything this stupid or chauvinistic. Like Lily said, it's a prank!"

A prank that could ruin him if the remarks were ever published, Anne thought. She felt even more distressed about her inadvertent part in this.

Home Free

"I see," the reporter mused, looking around at the stunned, anxious faces of the campaign workers. "Well, maybe I can use it, anyway."

"Wait a minute," Lily said desperately, in an attempt to save the day. "You heard John. You know this was all a stupid mistake. You're not going to print that—"

"Why not? The ineptitude of any campaign makes a great column."

John tried to talk him out of it, but to no avail. The reporter left, determined to make the mistake as public as possible. His temper in high gear, John stalked into his office and shut the door, very, very softly. Lily followed. Feeling as if she was about to be sick, Anne sat at her desk, deliberating. She knew she had to go in there, too.

"Who the hell sent out those press releases?" John thundered just as Anne eased her way into his office. She shut the door softly behind her.

"It—it doesn't matter," Lily said, avoiding Anne's glance.

"I sent out those press releases," Anne said, her knees trembling as she faced his wrath. The look he gave her was so grim and forbidding she gulped.

"And you didn't check each envelope to see what was inside?" he queried, dumbstruck.

"Yes, at first, but then—" she floundered, knowing as he did there was no excuse for her ineptitude. "I was in a hurry. There were a lot to go out. They were all the same." She hung her head in shame. "I'm sorry." Her hand shading her eyes, she whispered hoarsely, "I don't know how I could have been so stupid."

John was silent. He jerked at the knot of his tie and turned away, so he was staring out the window. Anne knew what he was thinking. *All that work, and now it was going to go down the drain, and why? Because his lover had just made a careless mistake that could cost him the election, that was why.*

She had never meant to hurt him. She would cut off her own arm rather than wound him in any way.

"I'll take the heat for this," she said quietly, knowing in her heart what the situation demanded she do. Determined to be strong for just a little while longer, she blinked back her tears. "I'll talk to the press. I'll explain it was all my fault and that you had nothing to do with it."

John remained silent, his head bowed in defeat.

It really is over, Anne thought, more depressed and dejected than she ever had been in her life. She walked back out to her desk, sat down and began typing her resignation.

Chapter Eleven

"Anne, wait, you can't just resign!" Lily said, following her. Aware of the grave damage she had done to John's campaign, other campaign workers were silent. "That's not what John wants!"

The truth was Anne didn't want to give up seeing John every day, either. But she also knew, even if Lily didn't, that it was time she left. Plans for the party were virtually all made. Lily could take over. Her quitting would vindicate John, and she had her ten thousand dollars. She could help a lot of people with that money at her agency. She could give Trong's case the full attention it deserved.

"Don't you see?" she asked, forcing herself to be practical. "Someone has to be the scapegoat. Since I made the mistake, it's only fair it be me. It's the only way to clear John's name and do so quickly, before any further damage is done."

Lily looked even more distressed. Unable to meet Anne's eyes directly, she mumbled with difficulty, "I guess you're right."

Turning, Lily went back into John's office.

Anne left as quickly as she could. She was still feeling tremendously guilty when John came by to see her later that evening. It was after eleven. She knew from watching him on the news that he'd spent the rest of the day explaining the gaffe to reporters. He had taken the crisis in stride and handled it in a calm, professional manner, but she knew there were voters out there who would remember only what he had supposedly said, not that it had all been a mistake.

"I needed to see you," he said simply when she'd opened the door. Although his voice was calm and patient, his eyes were not. They radiated hurt, anger, and fierce sexuality and desire that made her catch her breath.

I needed to see you, too, Anne thought, ushering him in wordlessly and shutting the door behind them. Although it was late, she'd been unable to summon the energy to get ready for bed. She was still dressed in white shorts and a navy-and-white boat-necked top. "I'm surprised you'd want to see me," she murmured as she led the way into her living room.

"Don't talk like that."

"Why not?" she asked quietly. "It's true. I may have cost you the governorship."

As honest and forthright as always, he couldn't deny what they both knew was true. "It was a mistake. An accident."

"Unfortunately that doesn't change the outcome or alter the facts."

"Don't you understand?" he asked huskily, his expression determined. "None of that matters. I love you. I'm not giving you up."

Tears flooded her eyes. "I only wish it were that simple," she whispered. He felt this way now, but how would he feel if he did lose the election because of her mistake or the scandal surrounding Tim? She couldn't bear it if he hated her. That would happen eventually; she knew it. Sooner or later he would blame her for this mess. Or his family would. Or the press would. One way or another, they would be miserable. And she couldn't bear it after what they'd had.

"It is that simple. I won't ever be happy without you," he whispered passionately. He framed her face with his hands, then tunneled his fingers through the silk of her hair. "You need me, too, Annie. We both know it in here." He took her hand and placed it on his chest, over the region of his heart.

Yes, Anne did know it. But that didn't mean her presence was good for him or his campaign. She tore her eyes from his. "I won't hurt you again," she insisted stubbornly, turning her head to the side. Why was he making this so difficult for her, dammit? Didn't he know how much it was costing her to be noble and do what was best for them all?

"You're hurting me now," John countered, just as passionately.

They argued a while longer. Finally John saw she wasn't going to change her mind. "The office isn't going to be the same without you," he said quietly, looking as utterly miserable as she felt. "I'm going to miss seeing you," he said sadly, holding her close.

I'll miss seeing you, too. More than you know. If he continued holding her much longer she really would break down and sob, so Anne wedged distance between them. Fighting back tears, she worked to keep her expression calm and self-effacing. "Who knows," she suggested lightly, "maybe you'll get more work done."

He gave her a long, hard look, letting her know her drollness fooled neither of them. "I doubt it," he said heavily, then looked away. After a pause, he sighed and said, "At least we have a long weekend coming up." He turned to her expectantly. "The whole family is going out to the Westfield compound for the Fourth."

Anne froze. She feared she had an idea what was coming next and in her current state of mind, an invitation like that was the last thing in the world she needed.

"It's my turn to host the party. I want you to be there with me, cohosting it. I want everyone to know how serious I am about you."

The last gathering had been frightening enough. The thought of facing John's grandmother after what she'd done to his campaign was even more terrifying. She also wasn't sure that she wanted to be the unmarried equivalent to John's political wife. Not if it meant giving up her career, the way Melinda had, or constantly putting herself in situations where she felt uncomfortable. "John—"

"It'll be fine," he stressed, impatient with her growing wariness.

No, Anne thought, it wouldn't be fine. Just anticipating the event, she felt a hot ache of tension in her stomach, rubbery knees, cotton mouth and burning cheeks. After all she'd been through the past few weeks, she was in no shape for this.

"John, I can't cohost the party with you." She paused and wet her lips, not liking the lack of respect she saw on his face. She forced herself to be as forthright as she could, "I'm not even sure, at this point, that I can go."

His face darkened. His disappointment in her was evident. "You mean you won't," he said angrily.

Anne was silent. His terse words hurt her, but that about summed it up.

John dropped his head. He let out a slow, unhappy breath, raked a hand through his hair and stood. His face was a formidable mask of pain. "I was married once to a woman who refused to become part of my world. I can't do it again, Anne." His mouth compressed grimly. "Life is too complicated without the two of us being drawn apart by your unwillingness to change."

His shifting the blame solely to her made her furious. She wasn't only doing this for herself, but for him. "What about your unwillingness to accept me as I am?" she cried. She was determined to get it all out in the open now that they'd started. She stalked closer. "If you care about me as much as you say you do, you've got to accept my limitations. Face it. I'm just not as social as you are, and I'm damn sure not as politically astute." She spread her hands wide. "I panic when I'm around your family."

He tucked a strand of hair behind her ear and encouraged gently, "You wouldn't have to feel frightened if you'd just let yourself get to know them better."

Frustrated, Anne turned away. She paced back and forth. "Before or after they eat me alive, John?" She stalked to the window and stood staring out. Her mind went back to the family picnic. Her feelings of inadequacy deepened. "You forget," she said softly, turning around to face him, "I met your grandmother. I know what kind of woman she thinks you need in your life. It isn't me."

John's expression remained impassive. "Gran has no say in who I fall in love with."

Anne lifted a dissenting brow. "Considering what I just did to your campaign, maybe she should."

John stared at her in frustration, knowing he wasn't going to get anywhere with her. He closed the distance between them and took her by the shoulders. "Look, I know how devastated you were by what happened. I was upset, too. But I'm not going to let one stupid incident ruin our life together and neither should you, Anne."

She feared that the warmth of his touch would seduce her into agreeing with him unwisely. She stepped away. "Meaning what?" she asked stiffly.

"Meaning if you love me as much as your kisses tell me you do," he said softly, taking her into his arms once again, "you'll forget all this nonsense, put aside your fear of not belonging and your feelings of inadequacy, and cohost the party with me."

"And if I don't?" She splayed her hands between them to successfully hold him at bay.

John shrugged, wishing the answer weren't so plain or so hard. "Then what kind of future do we have, Anne?" he asked.

Not much of one that he could see.

"JOHN'S CAMPAIGN is in big trouble, isn't it?" Carl asked when Anne dropped by to see her parents the following morning. She wasn't sure why she was there, only that she needed family around her, now more than ever.

"What with the scandal involving his brother's illegitimate son and now that letter that came out of his campaign—" Celia said, shaking her head in commiseration. She gave her daughter a look of heartfelt sympathy, then got up to pour them all some coffee. "Was John very angry with you?"

"He understands that it was an honest mistake," Anne said quietly.

"So what next?" her father asked.

"I'm going back to work for Answers, Inc. full-time."

Her parents weren't surprised. "What about your financial situation?" Carl asked cautiously. "I know you were scrambling for money before you took the job with John."

"All that's been solved. I received a sizable donation a few days ago. Ten thousand dollars, as a matter of fact."

"Darling, that's wonderful. Why didn't you tell us?" her mother asked.

"Because the money came from Robert Ryan." Her parents looked at her blankly. She took a deep breath, realizing she should've told them sooner. "My natural father."

The room suddenly became very quiet. Anne watched as the color drained from her adoptive parents's faces.

"You found him and didn't tell us?" Celia said, her hurt evident.

"I didn't know how. Not that it matters in the end, anyway." Anne got up to restlessly pace the room. "He denied being related to me. He said he had proof that his real daughter was dead and refused to look at anything to the contrary."

"Oh, honey, I'm sorry," Carl said numbly.

So am I, Anne thought, aware all over again how very much Robert Ryan's rejection had hurt.

"I wish it had turned out differently for you," Celia said after a moment, tears glimmering in her eyes.

"But you're not surprised, are you?"

Carl and Celia exchanged a look. "No," Celia said finally, her hand trembling a bit. "I guess I'm not—"

"You have to admit it was a terrible shock for him," Carl offered.

"Honey, we're sorry," Celia added. "We just don't know what else to say."

Neither did Anne.

Finally Carl cleared his throat. "Has your experience made a difference in the way you feel about your business?"

Anne glanced up in surprise. Sensing that some sort of confrontation was coming, she braced herself emotionally. "What do you mean?"

Carl sized her up in the way only a father could. "Are you going to go back to it?"

Clearly no harm had been meant in the remark, but Anne felt her hackles rise, anyway. "Of course. I have to."

"Do you?"

Anne's pulse started a heavy beat. "What are you getting at, Dad?"

Sensing a pending disaster, Celia jumped in, "Your father and I...we wonder if maybe it isn't time for you to pass the torch on.... Let someone else do the searching so you can get on with your own life, especially now that your own search has ended."

"We want to see you happy, Anne," her father added. "We want to see you put the past behind you and get on with your life. Maybe that would be easier if you weren't constantly conducting searches for other Amerasians," Carl finished gently.

"Look, I know you mean well, but Answers, Inc. is not interfering in my life."

"Isn't it? What about the situation with Tim Westfield? It seems that case alone has caused you a great deal of grief."

"I agree it was complicated, Dad, but it wasn't my fault."

Carl frowned, annoyed she wouldn't see his point and unwilling to let it go. "If you hadn't started the investigation—"

"Tim would have looked on his own, anyway," Anne interrupted hotly. She realized now that she hadn't come to fight with them, but to seek support and find a way to get closer to them. She wanted nothing, no one, not even Robert Ryan to stand in the way of their being the supremely close-knit family she had always yearned for. Determined to have them understand this, she swallowed and lowered her voice. "I knew the case was complicated. I knew it required diplomacy, tact and confidentiality. Tim's situation was very traumatic. When I found out about the scandal that had been suppressed, I tried to keep the information from him. And our efforts would've worked if not for the press."

Celia sipped her coffee without looking up.

"I know your intentions are good, Anne, that you think you're being noble, but it sounds to me like you're starting to play God with people's lives," her father said quietly. "And that isn't good, Anne."

Was she playing God? Anne wondered, flushing with renewed guilt. She hadn't meant to do so. She'd only meant to help Tim find the mother he'd been cruelly separated from. She bent her head in confusion and closed her eyes. What she should and shouldn't do with her life was no longer clear. Today, of all days, she had needed someplace where she could find unconditional love and understanding, the kind of love a child was supposed to get from her parents and the kind Robert Ryan had never given her.

"I came here looking for your support," she said, unable to suppress her hurt. Once again, she felt like an orphan. She got up abruptly, jarring the table. Coffee sloshed over the rims of all three cups and spilled. Tears streamed down her face. Inside, she felt more lost and alone than ever. "I guess I came to the wrong place."

"Anne," Celia interjected. "Don't go without giving us a chance to talk this out. Please. We just don't want to see you hurt. We don't want to see you act rashly or hurt anyone else, even inadvertently. Not like Tim was hurt."

Melinda had hurt Tim, Anne thought. She whirled on her parents. "Is that all you think I'm doing? Acting without thinking? Messing with people's lives for the hell of it? What about all the times I've helped people? Doesn't that count for anything?" Would she never measure up, in anyone else's eyes or her own?

"Of course it does," her mother was quick to reassure. "It counts a lot, Anne. We're very proud of you and your success."

"But we also know," her father added solemnly, "that it's a risky business. You're dealing with people's hearts. And it's taken its toll on you. We're not telling you to give up the cause. It's a good one, one that needs to be continued. We're just saying maybe *you've* been in it long enough," he said gently, his eyes kind. "Maybe it's time for you to start thinking about getting married, having a family of your own, and a life outside of your business."

"Like Leslie?" Anne cited her successful *married* older sister. She shook her head in bitterness and confusion. "Why do people always expect me to behave like someone else?"

"Anne, please," her mother cried, "you're not listening to us. You're taking this all wrong."

Was she? Anne thought about Robert Ryan's rejection of her and his attempt to send her a check and get rid of her that way. She thought of her own parents' attempt and even John's to push her into some cookie-cutter mold of the successful American woman that just didn't fit. She sighed in despair, knowing it would never work. She'd never live and breathe politics the way John and his family did. She'd never be able to give up her work or be the dutiful political wife. She'd never be Leslie or anyone else. All she could be was herself, and maybe it was just time she accepted the hard reality of her situation. She was on her own, alone, and always would be.

"I HEARD about Tim running away," Melinda said early one evening the following week, after stopping by John's house to see him. "I'm sorry."

John motioned to the sofa. He walked over to switch off the television. He cast his ex-wife a disparaging glance. It didn't help his morale any to notice she looked as bad as he felt. "You should be sorry," he said softly. He let his gaze bore into her. "You hurt all of us." Especially Tim.

Home Free

Melinda touched a hand to her thick red hair; her ivory skin looked even paler than usual. She lifted her blue eyes to his, grimacing apologetically. "I doubt it'll make you feel any better, but I've learned from the situation." She sighed and got up to pace the room restlessly. "Getting ahead at someone else's expense isn't worth it. I haven't been able to sleep much."

"Neither have I," John admitted, though his lack of sleep had more to do with his doomed relationship with Anne than his nephew. "Tim is a strong kid, though. He'll get over it."

Melinda nodded, apparently having come to the same conclusion herself. "What about you?" she asked, concerned. "I saw you've taken a nosedive in the polls."

John nodded grimly. One hell of a nosedive. The press just wouldn't let up on the bogus press release. They wouldn't let up on the fact that he'd hired Anne, then become romantically involved with her.

Melinda attempted to comfort him. "At least you got rid of the staffer who made the mistake."

Knowing his feelings were too close to the surface on that subject, John turned away. "I didn't get rid of Anne," he said, unable to help the harshness in his voice. "She resigned." He sighed. "And I didn't want her to do that."

Melinda studied him quietly. After a moment, she said, "You really care about her, don't you?"

"Yes," John said gruffly. "I do." But he was no longer sure it was going to work out. The entire incident had turned Anne off politics, and hence off him.

It had made her question her willingness to adapt to the political life-style. He'd called Anne repeatedly, but she had her machine on and she wasn't returning his calls.

"She must feel pretty embarrassed."

"More distressed than embarrassed. She's just upset that it happened, as am I." He exhaled slowly and shook his head. "She was stretched to the limit, working two jobs, trying to keep everything going. Even so, I just can't imagine her doing something that careless."

"But she says she did it?" Ever the journalist, Melinda continued to prod.

John nodded, his mood grim.

Melinda sighed and shook her head, looking as troubled as he felt about the situation. "What I don't get is why that release was still around," she mused problematically. She sent him a brief, incredulous look. "Didn't your staffers know enough to destroy it the minute the gag was over?"

"Of course they did." Without warning, John remembered the afternoon it had happened. Lily had brought the bogus press statement back into the office and read it to him. Then she wadded it up and threw it into the waste can beside his desk. He had seen her destroy the press release himself.

"And there was only the one copy."

John nodded, frustrated. He and Lily had been through this one hundred times since the crisis, to no avail. They still had no idea how the bogus statement had gotten mixed with the papers Anne had been sending. He didn't want to think it was a deliberate attempt to discredit him by one of the many volunteers or paid staffers working on his campaign, but the facts said otherwise.

Melinda raised her brow thoughtfully. "Looks like you have a saboteur in your midst."

Surely there was an answer to this. Surely someone must have seen or heard something. Maybe if he could *prove* to Anne that this hadn't been a mindless screw-up on her part, but a deliberate ploy, she would feel differently. Maybe that would prompt her to see that she should consider a life with him once again. It was a flimsy hope, he admitted, but it was the only one he had.

Melinda watched him grab his keys and wallet.

"Where are you off to?"

"Lily's." John's answer was short. If anyone knew the nitty-gritty about his headquarters, it was her. "We've got a lot to figure out."

"IS THIS A BAD TIME?" As anxious as he was to talk to Lily, he didn't want to interrupt a date.

"Not at all. Come on in." She motioned for him to make himself at home. "Can I get you something to drink?"

"No, thanks." John glanced at the typewriter. Still in the clothes she had worn to the office, she had obviously been working when he knocked. For a moment he pitied her. She was so tied to the office and her job. He looked at her again. "I wanted to talk to you."

"About what?" Lily smiled.

John felt vaguely uncomfortable. He had not been to Lily's apartment since right after his divorce to Melinda. He didn't remember it feeling confining or overly intimate then, but it sure felt so now. Nonetheless, he made himself sit down and attempt to make himself look at home. "It's about Anne. About what happened."

Lily's mouth thinned, but she recovered her professional cool. "Okay."

"I still don't understand how that memo got in the pile of press releases Anne was sending out."

Lily's eyes glazed over and she looked at him helplessly. "I don't know, either."

"Who gave her the press releases?"

Lily was silent. She looked uncomfortable again and very young. "I did." Two spots of color flared in her cheeks.

"Did you check them out first?"

Her head lifted sharply. "What are you implying?" she asked, a defensive note coloring her low voice.

John didn't know exactly. His gut feeling said there was something more. "I saw you throw that initial memo away," he said. "So one of two things happened. There had to be another copy of it or someone resurrected the original."

Lily was looking a little green around the gills. John hated upsetting her. Especially when he knew that she felt ultimately responsible for what had happened. She'd said so on more than one occasion.

"You're sure you don't want a drink?" Lily asked. She turned her back and headed for the kitchen. "I think I'm going to have some lemonade. It's been a long evening. My throat is parched."

"Okay." Impatient to sort this out, John started to follow Lily. As he did so, he moved past the short hall that led to Lily's bedroom and bath. He didn't mean to look but the door was open and he couldn't help it. A large framed photo of himself rested on the night table beside her bed. Dumbstruck, he stopped and stared. When he turned around, he saw Lily coming toward him, a glass of lemonade in her hand. She was waiting on him, again, the way a wife waited on a husband or vice versa. A chill went down his spine.

"I thought you might want some of those honey-roasted peanuts you're so fond of," Lily was saying. The cheerful note in her voice faded. She thrust the glass and bowl of peanuts at him. "I'll just shut this." She reached for the bedroom door.

John put the dishes on the coffee table. "Lily." She was so young, too young. Just twenty-three. He didn't know how to broach this without hurting her feelings, but he knew he had to ask. "What are you doing with a picture of me on your bedside table?"

Lily flushed bright red and didn't answer. And suddenly to John, so many things became very clear. The fact she was too attached to her job and perhaps to him. The fact she had no personal life. The fact for all their on-the-job intimacy, he didn't really know her at all. But she knew him, down to what snacks he preferred.

He swallowed hard, hoping he hadn't made a very big mistake when he hired her. "Is that a part of the campaign?" he continued, talking about the picture of him she had propped up next to her bed. If it was, he didn't consider it very healthy.

Her spine stiff, Lily did an about-face and walked back toward the kitchen, her hips swaying provocatively. "Let's just forget you saw that, okay?" Her voice was light, offhand.

But John couldn't forget it.

"As far as the bogus press release goes," Lily said when she returned with her own glass of lemonade in hand, "what difference does it make how it got into Anne's hands? The fact is she sent it out." Accusation echoed in the room. Lily sighed. Whether it was with relief or satisfaction John couldn't be sure. "And now she's gone. It's over."

Was it? John knew it wouldn't ever be for Anne. It had caused her to rethink her whole relationship with him. And he knew from the evasive way Lily was behaving that Lily wasn't telling him the truth, or at least not all of it. "You're not sorry she's gone, are you?" he asked. "You're not sorry she's out of my life?"

Lily shrugged and for once didn't pull any punches. "She wasn't right for you. We all knew that."

And who is, Lily? John wondered. He felt hurt and betrayed by the unexpected callousness of his trusted assistant. You? His thoughts returned to his picture on Lily's night table. He thought about the lack of romance in her own life and the fierce way she generally guarded him, screening out all the annoyances she could. And yet, not once in the whole bogus press release fiasco, had she ever gotten really upset.

Yes, she'd been distressed, but unlike him she hadn't raged about how it could have happened. Rather, she just seemed to have accepted that it had. In retrospect he found that a little strange. Shouldn't this whole mess have driven her just as crazy? he thought, perturbed.

Having seen enough, he set his glass and the bowl down. "I'm going to start my own in-depth investigation tomorrow morning. I'm going to find out who planted that memo if it's the last thing I do."

Lily looked distressed. "Why?"

"Because it's important," John said heavily. "I've got to know who betrayed me."

"Can't we just go on, like it never happened?" Lily pleaded.

How, John thought, when it's all but destroyed my romance with Anne? Unless he could prove her innocence in the matter, he would never salvage their relationship. "Just have the staff ready for questioning tomorrow morning," he ordered. "I'll take them into my office one by one and grill them personally. Someone is bound to have seen or heard something. Either that or they'll act guilty and give themselves away in that manner." He started for the door.

"Wait a minute," Lily protested, looking even more panicked and distressed. "You can't be serious. John! You'll destroy all morale if you do something like that. Think about the publicity! Your campaign can't take any more scandal."

"I don't care. Someone there betrayed me, Lily. I'm going to find out who and when I do—"

He hadn't even finished the sentence when she began to tremble. She turned away quickly. Wordlessly he watched her pace the room. "Don't," she said.

He followed her, able to feel in his gut that he was finally getting close to the truth. If anyone knew what had happened, it was Lily. She was just afraid to tell him. Maybe because she'd been involved? The mere thought seemed disloyal considering how devotedly she had served him over the past three years. But it was on target, and his own mood grim, he waited for her to come clean.

When she did, it hit him fiercely. "I—I wanted to get rid of her," Lily confessed tearfully at last. "I—I saw what she was doing to you, distracting you, and then when Tim and Gloria got hurt, too, I knew I had to act."

"By ruining my campaign?" John volleyed back incredulously, unable to believe she'd been so foolish and shortsighted.

Lily shrugged helplessly. "There's been so much talk about responsible journalism that I never figured a reporter would really print anything. I just figured Anne would get fired because of it. Please, John, you've got to forgive me."

He stared at her, his gut twisting. How could he have misread the signs for so long? She was in love with him, or she thought she was. "Lily," he said tiredly, realizing all over again what a child she still was at heart.

"I never meant to hurt you, either politically or personally," Lily sobbed, holding on to his shirt as she begged his forgiveness. "I swear it."

John knew that. Unfortunately it didn't diminish the suffering her actions had caused.

Chapter Twelve

"You've been avoiding me," John told Anne the last week in June when he stopped by her house. Not that he'd been easy to catch up with himself. His new assistant had booked him nonstop, in Concord and in various cities and towns around the state.

Anne went back to the letter she'd been typing on behalf of one of her clients. Finished, she rolled the paper out of the machine and put it on her desk. "Considering the dip you've taken in the polls, I thought it best if we didn't see each other. Or talk. Or—or anything."

He had figured that was the case. Noting that she'd lost both weight and sleep since they had split up, just as he had, he took her wrist and guided her unwilling body across the room, to sit on the sofa with him. She sat on one end; he sat on the other. The middle cushion stretched between them like the Grand Canyon.

"I wanted to tell you about Lily. You were set up, Anne." Briefly he explained to her how Lily had mixed

Home Free 233

in the bogus release with the real press releases. To his disappointment, Anne didn't feel vindicated.

She seemed in danger of dissolving into tears, but struggled laudably to remain composed. "I should have carefully inspected every paper, instead of just quickly folding them and inserting them into the envelopes I typed."

John took one of her hands between his and gave it a squeeze. "Hindsight is always better, Anne. You've got to stop beating yourself up about that."

Looking unconvinced, Anne withdrew her hand.

He paused, searching for a way to get through to her. "Besides, there are still five months until the election. I've got plenty of time to catch up."

"Provided," she said quietly, "there are no more mistakes."

"Even if there are mistakes," he said thickly, "I miss you."

"I miss you, too," Anne admitted. She closed her eyes, feeling anew the agony of being away from him and of no longer being a part of his life. "But I can't do what you want—"

He continued to scrutinize her, a shadow passing over his face. "Forget about cohosting the Fourth. I realized that was too much to ask and I—"

"Don't," she said, cutting him off. "We both know what you need in a wife, and I'm not it. At best, I have a controversial background. At worst, I screwed up your campaign, might have cost you the election, and am uncomfortable around your family. I love you and that will never change. You know that, but we have to be practical here. It's never going to work."

She didn't want him looking back, thinking how different his life would've been had he only married someone more suitable. And like his grandmother said, he'd already been divorced once. As a politician, he couldn't afford any more "mistakes."

Forgiveness was crucial to their happiness, but she couldn't seem to forgive herself. That frustrated him deeply. "I still want you to come to our July Fourth picnic at the compound." He removed an invitation from his pocket. His eyes searched hers. Maybe it was crazy, but he couldn't give up the hope that everything would still work out for them. "This will get you past the guards at the front gate. My whole family's going to be there—"

"Even Tim?" she interrupted, hoping that was so.

"No." John's despair over that mixed with Anne's. "He's still in Canada. Gloria invited him, of course, but he's angry and hurt. He feels betrayed. I guess it's going to take a lot of time."

Anne was silent John had tried to warn her not to look into Tim's case, but she hadn't listened. Because she hadn't, Tim had met his mother and been driven to find his father, and the Westfield name had been dragged publicly through the mud. If she had handled it better, maybe the scandal could have been avoided. But it was too late now to look back.

"You can bring your family, too," John continued softly, persuasively.

Anne got up and walked restlessly away from the couch. She threaded her hands through her hair. "John, it's over."

"It doesn't have to be," he argued, getting up to stand beside her.

"Yes," she retorted firmly, "It does."

John sighed. He wanted to touch her, pull her into his arms and kiss all her fears away. But he knew it would only be a temporary fix. They couldn't go on physically loving each other if they couldn't support each other emotionally, too.

Maybe Anne was more like Melinda than he knew. Loving someone took courage. As much as he wanted to, he couldn't give her that. It had to come from within.

"YOU CAME ALL THE WAY to Canada just to see me?" Tim asked, several days later.

Anne nodded, feeling as though she was getting herself on track again and doing what needed to be done. Softly she admitted, "I feel responsible for your being here."

Tim looked fit and healthy for the weeks he'd spent working outdoors. He arched a dissenting brow. "You're not responsible, Anne. If anyone is, it's my father." He gave a short, sardonic laugh. "Not that he's here to care."

Anne didn't know what to say. Tim missed his father. They might have been able to work things out if Frank had still been alive. Frank could have explained and somehow reassured his son that he had been dearly loved. But Frank wasn't here. And neither was Gloria nor John. Somehow, Anne had to find a way to get Tim back to the Westfield fold. She owed John's family that. And maybe then she would be able to rest, too. "Your family misses you, Tim. They want you back."

Tim shrugged. "I don't feel like I belong there anymore, you know?"

Unfortunately Anne did know. Before now, Answers, Inc. had been her first and only real priority. Now, being there only reminded her of all she had lost. The truth was supposed to set them free, but all it had done for Tim was to rob him of his respect for his father. She'd lost her dream of love and acceptance from her own father. She had been driven and full of purpose, but now she was lost and drifting, just as Tim was. "Tim, you can't keep on hiding from life. You've got to face your family and find a way to get on with it. They want you there for the Fourth. I think you should go."

Tim thrust his hands into the pockets of his khaki shorts. His jaw clenched stubbornly. "Even if I can't forgive what my father did?"

Anne looked into his dark eyes and tried to find a way to help him. Again, honesty seemed the only path. "I know what Frank did wasn't great, Tim, but you have to remember he did it out of love for you. Yes, he made a mistake, but he tried to rectify it. That's all that's important now." Tim looked unconvinced. "He risked everything to bring you back to the States, Tim. He could have lost his family and his future political career. That has to count for something." She dropped her voice a persuasive notch. "You still have a mother and three sisters who love and miss you."

And I have adoptive parents who love me, too, Anne thought with a mixture of guilt and regret. Maybe it's time I made peace with them, too. So what if we don't agree on everything? So what if Robert Ryan doesn't love me? Carl and Celia do. And heaven knew, they had been more parents to her than he ever had. One argument about her returning to Answers, Inc. shouldn't cancel out all that.

"You can choose to belong or not," she continued sternly. "Your family isn't doing this to you. They aren't ostracizing you. You're doing it to yourself."

"How's THE SPEECH going?" Gloria asked. She brought a fresh pot of coffee into the second floor library where John had holed up.

"Slowly," John said. At the moment, he couldn't concentrate on anything, never mind a speech about the significance of the Independence Day holiday. July Fourth was the last thing he wanted to think about. His every waking moment was filled with thoughts of Anne and the sometimes wonderful, sometimes exasperating love they had lost. Funny, it had taken him years to find the woman he wanted to spend the rest of his life with, but only a few weeks to lose her forever. Why? Because he hadn't found a way to make her feel secure. He hadn't found a way to make her feel loved.

That wasn't just because she was adopted or had been abandoned by her natural father. It was because she'd started out her life in another part of the world, in another culture, and because she still remembered what it was like to be Vietnamese. As a young child, that culture had been just as much a part of her security as her mother's love.

All that had changed when her mother died. Anne had ceased to belong anywhere but an orphanage. Had it not been for Carl and Celia and the generous hearts of the many Americans who had worked to bring the Amerasian children to the U.S., who knew what would've become of Anne?

If only he could make her and everyone see that it wasn't the color of one's skin or hair or the shape of one's eyes that made them American, but what was in their heart. It was having the courage to stand up for what was right, even in the face of great adversity and at great personal risk. It was having the tolerance and openness of heart, to be curious about other customs and cultures and embrace them. It was being generous, being the first to volunteer in times of heartbreak and tragedy, wherever your help was needed. Most of all, being an American meant being free to be whoever you wanted and needed to be, regardless of personal pressure or public opinion.

John thought of the way Anne had scrimped to open her own agency and of the tireless way she worked to help others. Whether she realized it or not, no one was more American than she.

Gloria handed him a cup of coffee. "Things have been crazy the past few weeks, haven't they?" she asked with all the sympathy a veteran political wife had to offer.

And lonely, John thought, nodding. No matter how busy, driven and exhausted he was, he still missed Anne like hell. And he was beginning to realize he always would, no matter how much time passed.

Misreading the reason for his mood, Gloria continued, "I'm sorry you had to fire Lily."

John sighed. That was something else for him to feel guilty about. "I didn't fire her," he corrected. "She resigned." She had said she loved him too much to go on working for him, when she knew that he would never return that love. Under the circumstances, he'd agreed it was best if she resigned.

Gloria studied him, seeing much more than he would've liked. "You miss Anne, don't you?" she chided softly.

"Is it that obvious?"

"Yes. But maybe it's for the best. Face it, John, she was just too different to be a good political wife."

John had heard that from nearly everyone since the breakup. He put down his pen slowly. "First of all, I never wanted to be with Anne because I thought she could help me politically or because it might go over better with the voters if I were married. I wanted to be with her because I love her and she makes me feel good. Second, possessing the freedom to be different is what this country is all about. Anne has every right to speak her mind and fight for what she believes. The same as you and I do." And Anne was doing that amidst a lot of disapproval and constant financial hardship. He was doing what he believed in by running for office and choosing to spend his life helping the less fortunate.

Gloria shrugged and continued to play devil's advocate. "Nevertheless, the two of you come from very dissimilar backgrounds—"

"We're the same in here—" he palmed his chest "—where it matters."

Gloria's eyes glittered with romantic satisfaction. Too late, he saw she'd just been pushing him to articulate his real feelings. "Maybe it's time you told her that," she prodded softly.

He wanted to tell Anne how he felt, but he'd also created enough trouble for Anne the past few weeks. She was barely over the Lily fiasco. His feelings still torn between wanting Anne and wanting to protect her, he said, "Don't you think I would tell her that if I thought it would make a difference? Don't you think I've tried?" Frustrated, he pushed away from his desk and stalked to the windows overlooking the lawn. He shoved a hand into his back pocket. "The trouble is she's so damn stubborn—"

"Oh, and you aren't," Gloria interjected dryly.

Gloria was making this all sound so simple and it wasn't. "I tried to get her to come to the picnic and bring her family." He faced Gloria. "I even tried to manage a surprise for her." For all the good it was going to do Anne now, he thought, since she hadn't shown up.

"And?"

John shrugged. "She refused point-blank, saying it was no use for her to come." And in his darkest hours, he had begun to think maybe she was right. If only she'd give me a sign, he thought. If only I had some tiny reason to hope that we could still rise above our current difficulties and work things out. But he knew that was unrealistic of him.

Anne wasn't going to put herself back into the fire and fray again. If he were completely fair about it, he couldn't blame her. It was all his fault they were in this situation. He'd been selfish. He'd wanted to get to know her, and the only way that was possible was to make her a part of his political campaign. So he'd talked her into taking the job. He'd put Anne in a situation that had caused her embarrassment and pain.

Even if she did ever get to the point where she would forgive him for that, what did he have to offer her? Being married to a politician was a lonely, demanding business. The demands of his job had to take precedence over his personal life.

Anne needed constant, loving attention. Even at his best, he wouldn't be able to give her the secure, quiet life she deserved. He thrived on chaos and activity and got a charge out of pushing his way right into the thick of things. Anne didn't mind putting herself on the line to help someone one-on-one, but put her in a larger group and she was lost. She'd be miserable leading his kind of life. He didn't know why he was so hell-bent on putting her there, but he couldn't envision any real happiness without her. Maybe it was time he asked Anne to marry him, without asking her to assume any duties that normally went to political wives. After all, he was managing now without a wife, wasn't he? Who said he couldn't manage to continue to do so in the future? There was no reason on this earth why she couldn't love him and continue running Answers, Inc. He could use every resource at his disposal to help her do just that....

"You're never going to get over her, are you?" Gloria asked compassionately.

"No, I'm not," John said. And maybe, it was time he did something about it.

ANNE AWAKENED early, aware it was a holiday, but feeling none of the joy she should have felt. All she could think about were the people she had loved and the way she had alienated them. Without her family, she knew she could never be happy.

She also knew that she'd been chasing a dream that just wasn't going to come true. Robert Ryan was her biological father, but he wanted no part of her future. It was time that she, like Tim, accepted what had happened and went on with her life. It meant being grateful for what she had, not yearning aimlessly for what she didn't.

She got to Carl and Celia's before breakfasttime. They greeted her with surprise and trepidation. "Anne, darling, come in," Celia said.

"I know it's early—" both were still in their pajamas and robes "—but I wanted to talk to you."

"I'm glad you came." Her mother enveloped her in a hug and closed her eyes against the tears that threatened to fall. Anne hugged her back. It felt good to be home. It felt good to be loved. She had missed them. She hadn't realized until this moment how very much.

"I'm sorry we argued the other day," her dad said gruffly, giving her a hug, too.

"I'm sorry, too." Anne's vision was misty as she sat down at the kitchen table with them. She hoped they'd be able to forgive her for the way she'd hurt them.

"In retrospect, I think we were just hurt because you hadn't told us about Robert Ryan," Celia said.

Her dad nodded. "We all said a lot of things we didn't really mean. You have every right to continue working with Ameriasians, Anne."

She searched his face. "You mean that?"

Carl nodded. "You're the only one who can decide what's right for you. If that's it, so be it."

"Thank you. It means a lot to me to have your support. The other day I said a lot of things I didn't mean, too." She had difficulty going on; it took all her courage. "All these years I've felt cheated because I wasn't living with my natural mother and father. I felt my life would have been better somehow if I had been. I was wrong." Her mother's and father's eyes both filled with tears.

Anne shook her head sadly. She reached across the table, clasped both their hands and continued thickly, "No one could have loved me as much as you two did. No one." Her voice caught, but she forced herself to go on. "I know I've kind of forfeited my rights here, with my recent behavior—"

"Don't ever say that," her mother cut in fiercely, her voice as choked with emotion as Anne's. She got up, circled the table and gave Anne a fierce hug. "You're our daughter and you always will be."

"No matter what," her father added, getting up to hug her, too.

"Then I'm still a member of this family?" Anne asked, aware she had never needed and wanted her parents more.

"You better believe it!" Carl said, hugging her again.

At peace with that part of her life, at long last, Anne knew she had only just begun to get the whole of it back on track. "John asked me out to his family's compound, for their Independence Day celebration. I want to go and I want you to go with me."

Carl and Celia exchanged fretful glances. "We want to be with you—"

"We don't want to intrude—"

"John asked me to bring you."

"That's very kind of him, but, honey, we wouldn't know what to say around those people or even what to wear," Carl said.

Hearing someone else express the same doubts and insecurities she herself had felt made Anne realize how much she had grown. And all because of John. "It's okay. Just be yourself."

"Are you sure?" Carl and Celia looked unconvinced. They didn't want to embarrass her.

"Very." Anne smiled. For the first time in months, she felt as though she really belonged. Not because anyone had done anything to make her feel welcome, but because she wanted to belong. She wanted to stop living her life on the sidelines and join in. She smiled, adding gently, "This is America, after all. People are free to be anything and everything they want."

"HEY, ANNE, how's it going?" Tim asked when Anne entered the compound with her parents several hours later. She knew they were late. The festivities had started at ten, but the Westfields were such a laid-back clan that the three of them would be welcome whenever they arrived.

"You came back!" Anne was delighted to see Tim looking so good.

"Yeah. I knew it was time," Tim admitted abashedly. In the distance, a fife-and-drum corp struck up a spirited version of "Yankee Doodle Dandy."

Another chapter closed, Anne thought. She was delighted to see that the tents she had ordered were a beautiful, billowy white. The podium was decorated in patriotic red, white, and blue. Everywhere she looked, there were flags and streamers, festive reminders that it was indeed the Fourth of July. "Have you seen your uncle John?" Anne asked, more eager than ever to see him and find a way to mend the rift that had torn them apart.

"I think he's still up in his study, working on his speech. The press is showing up later, you know, to tape it for the evening news. Are these your folks?

Glad to meet you," Tim said gregariously, extending a hand. "Can I introduce you folks around...."

Leaving her parents in Tim's capable hands—his first order of business seemed to be to set them both up with some cotton candy and lemonade—Anne went in the direction of the house. She passed Margaret Westfield on the way. "My grandson's in a blue funk because of you!" Margaret said.

Anne didn't stop for the lecture Margaret apparently wanted to give. She no longer cared if John's grandmother or anyone else thought she was right for him. "That's about to change," Anne retorted, and the older woman grinned back at her show of spirit.

Francine was heading for the kitchen. "Hey, Anne, glad you made it! Don't suppose you want to help me supervise the caterers later on? They'll be here to start setting up for the evening meal soon."

"I'd be glad to," Anne said cheerfully. "But first things first and right now I've got to find John."

"Second floor." Francine pointed. "Take a left at the head of the stairs and go down the main hall, all the way to the end."

The upstairs was relatively quiet compared to the wealth of activity elsewhere on the rambling estate. Her heart pounding, Anne stepped over a discarded soccer ball, one roller skate and a baseball bat, and made her way down the main hall, to the end. *Please let him be there. Please let him still love me.*

The study doors were open. John was standing at the windows overlooking the lake. He turned at the sound of her footsteps. No emotion was readily discernible on his face.

"Anne—" he murmured. Days before his questioning look alone would have given her second thoughts, but not anymore. *I'm not going to let my own fear of failure stop me. I love him. I've got to try to make things work. And if this fails, I'll try again and again.*

"Don't say anything." She cut him off in a voice that trembled, afraid he would throw her out before she'd had a chance to make amends. She couldn't have lost him yet, she reassured herself, not when they had loved each other so much.

His head lifted. He remained silent.

She waited for the fear and insecurity she had felt for years to come. It didn't. Now that she was here, she felt strangely peaceful, content and secure. She was on the verge of having everything she wanted, at long last, if only she played her cards right.

She moved forward, into the square of sunshine where he stood. The lively sounds of children playing wafted in through the windows. Knowing it was now or never, she took a deep, gulping breath and looked up at him beseechingly. "I know I told you we were all wrong for each other. I know I said it would never work." She hesitated, fighting the tremor in her voice. "What I didn't know then was how very much I want to try."

John gave a sigh of relief. Reaching out, he reeled her into his arms and buried his face in the fragrant depths of her hair. The thundering beat of her heart matched his. "I want to try, too," he murmured fervently, holding her very, very close. After a moment, he drew back. "But not the way it was before."

Drinking in the strength and reassurance in his eyes, she knew everything was going to be all right.

"I was wrong to ask you to change your life to fit mine. I don't need a wife to campaign for me, Anne. I need a woman to share my life with, a woman to talk to late at night, a woman to hold in my arms and make love to, a woman who'll make love to me. I need you, Anne, and only you." He finished thickly, "And that's all I need."

"Oh, John, I need you, too," she whispered, knowing now that what they felt for each other made them strong. It would see them through whatever happiness, whatever storms, lay ahead. Finally her life was on track once again.

LONG MOMENTS LATER, John lifted his head. With delight, he announced, "I've got a surprise for you."

Anne couldn't imagine what it was. She already felt she had everything she needed. "What kind of surprise?"

Smiling enigmatically, he said, "You'll see." Taking her by the hand, he led her out of the house and across the lawn to the tennis courts. This time, as she passed Gran, Gran smiled and waved. "Looking better, Johnny," Gran called.

John gave Margaret the high sign. "Feeling better, too. A lot better!"

Anne saw Carl and Celia. They were playing croquet with Tim, Gloria and John's three nieces. "I almost forgot. My parents are here."

"Good." His hand tightened on hers as he paused to wave to her folks. "I want our families to know each other."

He stopped just short of the tennis courts. Anne saw Robert Ryan. He'd been seated on the sideline, watching the game. He stood and moved slowly toward her. John loosened his grip, as if to let go of her, but Anne held on to him more fiercely than ever. "You'll be fine," John whispered in her ear. He gave her a little push in Robert Ryan's direction. "Just talk to him."

That quickly, John was gone. Robert Ryan was beside her. They faced each other awkwardly. Behind them, the game went on nonstop.

"I hope you're not angry that I'm here," He began. He looked as nervous and ill at ease as Anne felt. "I wanted to come."

Anne dropped her eyes. Old hurts pressed in on her heart. She knew she should forgive him, but after the way he had treated her, it wasn't as easy as she would've hoped. "Why would I object?" she asked calmly. She forced herself to meet his eyes and see his sorrow, regret, and guilt.

"Because I was cruel to you," he said softly. "Because I didn't believe you."

The words Anne had longed to hear brought solace to her heart. He was a handsome man, and when he wasn't on guard, very kind. Beginning to see what her mother must have seen in him, Anne asked softly, "Why didn't you?"

Robert Ryan sighed, looking elegant and fit in his tennis whites. "Believing you would have made me feel guilty, Anne. It would have made me face my own inadequacy." Putting a hand on her shoulder, he led her farther away from the other guests, so they could talk more privately. "I loved your mother a lot, Anne, and even though you were just an infant when I left, I loved you, too. It broke my heart when I thought I'd lost you both." He spoke with gut-wrenching honesty; moisture shimmered in his eyes.

"But somehow, I managed to put it behind me and go on. When you showed up, my whole world came crashing down. I didn't want to believe you were still alive. That meant accepting the fact I had abandoned you, however inadvertently. I told myself it was a hoax, and that even if it wasn't, too much time had passed for us to mean anything to each other now." He sighed heavily. "So I gave you a donation, hoped that would buy you off, and tried to forget. But all along I knew that what you told me was true." He paused, all the sorrow and shame he felt showing on his face. "I'm sorry I hurt you." He swallowed with difficulty. "I'm sorry I wasn't there for you."

"What made you change your mind?"

"You," he said simply, his eyes filled with pride. "The way you wouldn't give up. Even after all those years. You just kept looking for me. And then there was John. He called me and told me that sooner or later I would have to deal with the truth whether I liked it or not. He said it was destroying you inside to be abandoned all over again and I knew he was right. I had to stop being selfish. The bond between us wasn't going to go away."

Tears flowed down his face and hers. Struggling to retain what little was left of her poise, Anne turned away. She had dreamed of this moment for so long, yet now she dreaded complications. "I still love my parents," she warned, her voice hoarse. As much as she wanted and needed to welcome Robert Ryan into her life again, she didn't want to hurt Carl and Celia.

"I know that." He reached over and squeezed her hand reassuringly. His dark blue eyes were kind and compassionate. "I don't want to interfere or try to take their place. I just want us to be friends." He hesitated. "Do you think that's possible?"

It was not only possible, it was ideal, Anne thought, and told him so.

John returned. "Everything okay here?" he asked, looking from one contented face to the other.

Anne nodded, the relief she felt encompassing her entire soul. "Everything's fine," she said.

"HAVE I TOLD YOU what a great Fourth this has been?" John asked as midnight approached. The two of them strolled down toward the lake.

"About a million times." Anne smiled as she linked hands with him. The food had been wonderful. His speech and the entertainment were great. The media had been impressed. "But you can tell me again."

John stopped walking. He drew her around to face him. "I could," he agreed softly, his gaze roving her upturned face, "but I'd rather show you." He bent toward her. Their lips touched. A thousand sensations ignited. Anne leaned into him, her breasts pressed against his shirtfront. Reveling in the way he made her feel, she wreathed her arms around his neck and drew him even closer. This was bliss, she thought, pure unadulterated bliss... the kind of bliss she had been yearning for and dreaming of as long as she could remember.

When the kiss ended long minutes later, Anne thought her life had never been so complete. But when she looked at John, she saw he was frowning.

"There's only one thing missing," he said.

Anne looked back at the lawn in alarm. From what she could see, everyone was having a marvelous time. They'd had old-fashioned sack races, apple bobbing, sparklers and music. Tim and his sisters were video taping the event.

"What could possibly be missing?" she asked in alarm. After all, it had been her job to organize the party.

John's frown switched to a grin. He lifted her left hand to his lips and kissed it gently. "A little gold ring here—" he kissed her left hand again "—and a matching one here." He pointed to his own hand.

Anne looked from his hand to his eyes. Was he leading up to what she hoped? As their gazes linked, she knew she had never felt such love. And with John in her life again, it was something she was going to have to get used to feeling.

"Marry me," he urged quietly, "just as soon as this election is over."

Her breath caught in her throat. "Oh, John—" she whispered happily. He kissed her again.

"I take it that was a positive response?" John murmured. His arms tightened possessively around her waist. In the distance, a brass band struck up "Stars and Stripes Forever." Fireworks exploded above them in the lush midnight-blue sky.

Anne looked up at him and grinned. What a glorious Fourth of July this had turned out to be! "Most definitely, that's a yes," Anne murmured back, knowing all her dreams had come true. She had the love of John and her family. And she was an American, with all the feelings of freedom and belonging that entailed, at last.

HARLEQUIN
American Romance

ABOUT THE AUTHOR

Cathy Gillen Thacker comes from a large, loving family. She grew up in Fairfield, Ohio, and did all the usual things American kids do. She joined the choir and the marching band and was a member of the student council and a class officer. She got good grades and went on to college.

Now married and the mother of three equally busy and involved teenage children, Cathy often wonders what would have happened to her had she not come from such a warm and sharing environment or had such loving and supportive parents. She wonders what would have happened had she grown up in another country or had parents who were of two diverse cultures.

In *Home Free*, Cathy looks at what it is to love and be loved, to have the sense of belonging that only your family can give you, and at what it really means to be an American today. Cathy hopes you spend your Independence Day celebrating your good fortunes with family and friends, as she will, this and every year to come.